novels
A Nest of Simple Folk
Bird Alone
Come Back to Erin

short stories
Midsummer Night Madness
A Purse of Coppers
The Man Who Invented Sin
The Finest Stories of Sean O'Faolain
I Remember! I Remember!

biography
Constance Markievicz
King of the Beggars
The Great O'Neill
Newman's Way

travel
An Irish Journey
A Summer in Italy
An Autumn in Italy

criticism
The Short Story
The Vanishing Hero

play
She Had to Do Something

translations
The Silver Branch

miscellaneous
The Irish

I Remember!
I Remember!

I Remember! I Remember!

stories by

Sean O'Faolain

an atlantic monthly press book
little, brown and company
boston   toronto

LIBRARY OF CONGRESS CATALOG CARD NO. 61-9053

FIRST EDITION

ATLANTIC–LITTLE, BROWN BOOKS
ARE PUBLISHED BY
LITTLE, BROWN AND COMPANY
IN ASSOCIATION WITH
THE ATLANTIC MONTHLY PRESS

Published simultaneously in Canada
by Little, Brown & Company (Canada) Limited

PRINTED IN THE UNITED STATES OF AMERICA

RIGOR VERIS AUTUMNO VERGENTE SOLUTUS

contents

I Remember! I Remember!   1

The Sugawn Chair   23

A Shadow, Silent as a Cloud   31

A Touch of Autumn in the Air   55

The Younger Generation   69

Love's Young Dream   83

Two of a Kind   121

Angels and Ministers of Grace   137

One Night in Turin   155

Miracles Don't Happen Twice   205

No Country for Old Men   213

I Remember!
I Remember!

I believe that in every decisive moment of our lives the spur to action comes from that part of the memory where desire lies dozing, awaiting the call to arms. We say to ourselves, "Now I have decided to do so-and-so," and straightway we remember that for years and years we have been wanting to do this very thing. There it is, already fully created, clear on the horizon, our longed-for island, its palm tree waving, its white hut gleaming, a brown figure standing on the beach, smiling patiently.

I am remembering Sarah Cotter and her infallible memory. If she were not so childlike, so modest, so meekly and sweetly resigned, she could be a Great Bore, as oppressively looming as the Great Bear. She can remember every least thing she ever heard, down to the last detail, even to the hour of the day when it happened. She is a Domesday Book of total recall for the whole of the little town of Ardagh, where she has lived for some twenty-five years in, you might almost say, the same corner of the same room of the same house, ever since an accident to her spine imprisoned her in a Bath chair at the age of eleven. This accident absolved her from all but the simplest decisions: there was no far-off island for her to dream of. It also meant that all she can now know of the world outside is what she reads, or what she is told by her friends, so that if her friends have told her fibs their consciences should prick them when she trustingly retails something that did not happen, or not quite in that way.

She is a little hunched-up woman with a face like a bit of burnt cork, whose plainness, some might say whose ugliness, you forget immediately you notice her gentle expression, her fluent lips, her warm brown eyes. Remember that, because of her ailment, she is always looking upwards at you when you meet her, so that her eyes have the pleading look of a spaniel, as if she were excusing herself for so much as existing. Her only handsome feature, apart from her doggy eyes, is her hair, long and rich and fair, on which she spends hours every morning, brushing it down into her lap over her shoulder, then brushing and pinning it up in a soft cloud, so overflowing that it makes her agile monkey-face seem about the size of a hazelnut. She lives in almost constant pain. She never complains of it. I have met nobody who does not admire her, nobody who has the least fault to find with her, apart from her invulnerable memory, which all Ardagh both enjoys and fears, and whose insistence can kill like the sirocco.

The only grumbles ever heard from her are two, as constant and soft as the leaves of a bamboo grove. The first is that she wishes she could see more of her sister Mary, a tall, slim, pretty, volatile girl, who twelve years ago married an American businessman, Richard Carton, a Continental buyer for one of New York's biggest stores.

"Not," she always adds, "that I don't realize how lucky the pair of us are. We mightn't be seeing one another atall only for Richard having that wonderful job."

Because of this job, a cablegram or a letter has come twice a year from Mary saying that Richard is off to Europe on another buying spree, which means that Mary will presently stop off at Shannon and drive over to Ardagh for a week of heavenly gossip. Sarah at once announces the news to the whole of Ardagh, with burning cheeks and sparkling eyes. Then she may murmur her other grumble:

"Imagine it! I've seen Richard only once in my life. If he wasn't so busy! If only he could come with Mary for a real long holiday! Then she wouldn't have to go away after one little week. But, of course, she's indispensable to him."

What she does not know, and what Mary intends that she never shall know, though she fears sometimes that one or two people in Ardagh may know it, or at least suspect it — such as Joe Shorthall, who picks her up at Shannon in his taxi, or the postmistress, who has sent off an occasional telegram for her — is that for the last six years Richard and she have been living partly in New York and partly in their small, elegant house in Zurich, near which their three children are at an English boarding school — so that, all unknown to Sarah, her sister passes between Switzerland and New York about six times a year. As for being indispensable to Richard in his work, the only time she ever ventured to advise him was in Rome. He looked at the object, a large, handsome blue fruit dish, turned it over and showed her the mark of its Californian manufacturer. What keeps her from visiting Sarah more often is the tireless whisper of the Recording Angel's Dictaphone playing back every lightest word that has passed between the two of them since they could begin to talk. She once incautiously wailed to Richard about it:

"It's not just that it's disconcerting to be reminded about things you've said, or discarded or forgotten years and years ago. Oh, if it was only that! She brings out these bits and scraps of things I've forgotten since I was ten, like a dog digging up some old thing you've thrown out on the ash heap and laying it lovingly at your feet — grubby, pointless, silly, worn, stupid things — and she says, 'That's you.' And I don't recognize them. Or don't want to see them. Old toys, old hats, old buried bones. Sometimes she has to remind me and remind me before I can even know what she's talking about. And, anyway, by this time they're no longer bits of me, they're bits of her. She knows more about me than I know myself. I keep on wondering what else does she know about me that I don't know. What's she going to produce next? Isn't my life my own, goddammit, to keep or to lose or to throw away if I want to? Am I me? Or am I her? I sometimes think I'm possessed by that old Chucklepuss the way some people are possessed by the devil!"

Richard had laughed heartily, and she, remembering too late his first, famous, fatal and final session with Sarah, could have bitten her tongue off. She stuck it out at him. Remembering again, he laughed all the more. Because Richard's memory is just as unerring as Sarah's; and his interest in Mary's past just as avid, or it used to be during the first years of their marriage. He wanted to know everybody she ever knew before he met her, every single thing she had ever done, every thought she had ever thought, every place she had ever been. So, at that first and last meeting between him and Sarah, she had to sit listening, apprehensive or embarrassed, while those two laid out the days of her youth before them like precious things that a pair of antiquaries might love to display to one another but would never part with. As they went on and on she got more and more furious with them:

"Ye make me feel like baby's first shoe. Or a photograph of a First Communion group. Or me aunt's wedding veil. Ye make me feel ninety. Ye make me feel dead!"

Richard only laughed his jolly, buyer's laugh, hangjawed like a pelican — worth thousands to him in his job — and roared at her to go away and leave them to it.

"This Sally girl knows tons more than you ever told me."

But how could she go? She was as fascinated as she was furious. She was also frightened. For, while Sarah did know, or remember, "tons more," it was all untrue in the way that a police report is untrue, because it leaves out everything except the facts. As she listened, transfixed as a rabbit is by a dazzling light that hides anything behind it, she remembered a wonderful thing she had once read in Stendhal's diaries — that "True feeling leaves no memory": meaning that every deep feeling is like a peach, to be eaten straight from the tree of life, not spoiled by pawing and pressing. She swore afterwards that she lost pounds in perspiration while listening to them. The worst sequence was when they started talking about Corney Canty:

"Sally!" she heard Richard saying suddenly. "Tell me about this young Corney Canty of Mary's. She's told me a lot about that wild boyo. As a matter of fact, why don't we meet him?"

"But, darling," Mary protested, "I've told you a dozen times over all that there is . . ."

"Now, Mary! Now! Let Sally tell me. Go on, Sally! Mary's told me about how they used to go riding to hounds together. And all the other adventures they had. That must have been a wonderful day — As I recall, Mary, it was the May of nineteen-thirty-seven? — when the two of you, alone with three hounds, flushed a fox out of Ballycoole woods and ran him to the edge of Gaunt's Quarry. And the brave Corney — He must really be a marvelous horseman, Sally — just slid after him down the gravel face of that quarry without a moment's hesitation. And poor little Mary here — Look at her, she's pale again at the thought of it! — God, how I admire you, darling! — terrified out of her wits though she was, slid down after him. And they cornered the fox in that quarry! I'd really love to meet this fellow. Why don't we ask him in for a drink tonight?"

Sarah's eyes dropped.

"God rest him!" she murmured.

"Not dead? Killed on the hunting field? A fine young man like that killed in the prime of life! Did you know this, Mary?"

"Did you say 'young,' Richard?" Sarah soothed him. "Sure when he died of the drink there a few years back he was seventy-two to the month."

"Seventy-two?" — looking wide-eyed at Mary, who was crying out desperately:

"Sarah, you're thinking of Corney's uncle. Or his father. He wasn't a year over forty, and as limber as twenty-five. Of course," gushing to Richard, "he was a great rascal, you couldn't trust a word he said, didn't I tell ye the time he deliberately made me fall off that gray mare of his, setting me to a stone wall he knew damn well she couldn't take, so that he could come around and kneel over me on the grass, feeling me here and feeling me there with 'Does it hurt here, ducky?' and 'Does it hurt there, ducky?', and me with the wind gone out of me so that I couldn't say a bloody worrrd!"

Richard laughed at the familiar story, one of his favorites that he liked to make her tell at every second party, because it brought out the brogue in her voice. Sarah was not to be silenced.

"He was," she said primly, even a little severely, "seventy-two years old to the month when he died. No more. No less. I myself witnessed his cross — he couldn't read or write — on the Old Age Pension form on December the first, nineteen hundred and forty-three. He was wearing that old red-flannel-lined raincoat your daddy gave him in thirty-seven when . . ."

"But," Richard put in, "that was the year of the quarry hunt."

"That's right. 'I have this coat,' said Corney to me, 'for six years, and your poor father had it for six years before that, and . . .'"

Mary could see by Richard's face — he could multiply 113 by 113 in his head — that he had already established for himself that "young Corney" had been an old lad in his middle sixties when she knew him. Sure enough, when Sarah paused, there was a brief silence, suspenseful and decisive, and then he broke into a series of monster guffaws, beating his palms together with delight, relishing with loving malice his wife's scarlet embarrassment. Through his guffaws he managed to utter:

"Mary, you little divil, I always knew you exaggerate a bit, but this . . ."

Wildly she fought for her hour as she had lived it:

"I didn't exaggerate. That was typical of Corney to exaggerate his age to get the pension. He fooled you up to the eyes, Sarah; when we hunted that fox he was forty, forty-two at the very most, forty-two at the outside limit, not a minute over it."

One glance from Richard's bubbling shoulders and wrinkled-up eyes to Sarah's prim mouth told her that the battle was hopeless. There Sarah sat, erect in her chair, too nice to contradict further, too honest to compound a felony, giving her head short little shakes that said as plainly as speech, "Seventy-two. To the month. No more. No less."

Neither then nor at any time after could Mary have understood that Richard was just as happy with her as a splendid Teller of Tales as he had been with her as his Wild Irish Girl. Blinded by love, he drew out the session for hour after hour. He only realized his folly that night, in the hour of tenderness, in bed.

"Dammit," she said, as they lay side by side, in her parents' old room upstairs, the heavy mirror in the coffinlike ward-

robe catching the last of the summer daylight, the faint
baa-ing of sheep coming from the Fair Green, "I did slide
down that old quarry. I wasn't codding about it. And he
wasn't an old man. And even if he was I think that makes
it a hell of a sight more exciting than the sentimental way
you want it. Handsome young Irish huntsman. Brave
young Irish girl. It makes me sick the way you always want
to romanticize everything about me."

His hands behind his poll, he began to shake all over
again until she started to hammer him with her fists on his
chest, and he to embrace and fondle her with a new love, a
new admiration — he said the words, just so, explicitly —
which, she declared, turning her behind to him huffily, was
entirely beyond her modest intelligence. She whirled, and
sat up and shouted:

"Are you trying to say that you prefer me as a liar?"

"Husssh! My wild little girleen! Sarah will hear you."

"I don't give a damn if she does hear me. What does she
know about it? She wasn't there. It was she started all this,
and you kept at her and at her to make me seem more of a
liar."

"Nonsense, darling. It's just that you have this wonderful Irish gift for fantasy."

"It's not fantasy. It's true, true, true. Every word of it is
true. There may be some detail here or there, some trivial,
irrelevant thing, some small thing slipped up, but it's all
true. And I am not going to have you and old Sarah
Sucklepuss down there stealing my life from me with her
bloody old . . ."

And, to his pitying astonishment, she burst into a long,
low wail of weeping, sobbing into the pillow like, he
thought, as he laid his palm on her wet cheek, a child whose
dog has been rolled over by a bus before her eyes.

"You don't understand, Dicky," she wailed into his armpit. "It's torture to hear her digging up my life and turning it all into lies that never happened the way she says they happened."

"But you must have told her they happened that way?"

"I told her the bones. And all she has of anything now is the bones. I can't remember the bones. All I have is the feeling I had at the time. Or else I can't remember at all."

"Tell her so. Say you forget."

"It would be like taking her life away from her. All the poor old Sucklepuss has is my bones."

She wept herself asleep on his shoulder. It is the measure of his distress at what he had done to her, of his natural shrewdness, and of his sensitiveness hidden behind his cocktail-bar laugh that as he lay there, listening to the dim, distant, ceaseless baa-ing, he decided never again to visit Ardagh.

But this was years ago, and since then Mary's life has stopped being the flowing, straightforward river it once was. Not that life ever is like a river that starts from many tributaries and flows at the end straight to the sea; it is more like the line of life on my palm that starts firmly and frays over the edge in a cataract of little streams of which it is impossible to say where each began. Richard has small interest now in her youth. He is rarely amused by her exaggerations: the wind that blew the legs off her, or the bus that went down Fifth Avenue at a hundred miles per hour. Her lovely, lighthearted, featherheaded ways are now her usual scattiness. She finds it more and more difficult to follow Sarah's letters about the latest doings of Ardagh. And the only way Sarah can form any clear pictures of Mary's life in New York is by those intimate gossips, prolonged into the silence of the night, during Mary's precious half-yearly visits to the little house near the end of the Main

Street of Ardagh. Yet, it was just when, for this very reason, one might have expected the visits to become either
more frequent or longer that they suddenly became so curt
that everybody but Sarah foresaw their end.

It all started out of a ridiculous little incident that occurred during Mary's March visit last year. Over the years
she had been trying in vain to free herself from Sarah's
memory by catching her out in an error of fact. On this
wet, March night she suddenly became aware that Sarah
was talking of a German air raid on a part of the Irish
coast where some old friends of Richard's, working in the
American diplomatic service during the war, had had a
summer house. Knowing well that no German bombs had
dropped on this part of the coast, she felt an overwhelm-
ing sense of relief. She did not contradict the Recording
Angel. She did not crow over her. She stayed as quiet as a
cat watching a mouse. The whole value of the error was
that Sarah must never become aware of it. The night
passed with the error uncorrected. At about two o'clock
in the morning Mary woke up as if to the sound of a shot,
remembering clearly that a floating sea-mine had exploded
on that part of the coast and damaged a summer house.
She left Ardagh the next day, only three days after she
had arrived, to Sarah's dumb dismay, on the feeble excuse
of being worried about Richard's health. ("Oh, Sarah, I
live in terror that he'll have to give up the job altogether,
he's driven *so* hard!")

Six months later, in September, Mary came again, and
left after two days.

They were having afternoon tea on the second day of
this visit — it was a Sunday afternoon — in the bay of the
front room, looking out on the empty autumn street, with
Sarah happily squeezing the last drops out of a long, lightly
amusing evocation of the famous night seventeen years

before when Mary, still at school, organized a secret Mid-
summer Eve party to hail the sun rising over the Galtee
Mountains. She had rowed her party, five in all, across the
river in the dark and lit a pagan midsummer-fire in, of all
places, the playing fields adjoining the Mercy Convent. The
nuns, rising to sing their Matins, had heard the singing and
seen the fire, and raised a terrible row about it, which set
the whole town talking for weeks after. Sarah happily
followed the history of everybody even distantly connected
with the affair down to the hour of that afternoon tea. Her
comments were largely a string of *Requiescats*, a ritual
habit which always secretly tickled Mary: it was as if the
Recording Angel had a secondary job as Lady High Ex-
ecutioner. ("Anna Grey? Died nine years back, Mary.
Tommy Morgan? Failing. Failing before his people's eyes.
Joe Fenelon took to the bottle, poor boy. Molly Cardew?
Ah, God rest her . . .") Without a pause Sarah leaned
forward and said:

"Mary, tell me! How is Nathan Cash these days?"

"Nathan who?" Mary had said, parrying wildly at the
unexpected transition. This sort of thing was always hap-
pening — Sarah suddenly producing some name or event
about which she was supposed to know nothing.

"Cash!" Sarah said loudly, rather like people who raise
their voices when talking to foreigners in order to be better
understood. "Your friend Nathan Cash. The man who was
a director of the Bell Telephone Company in Newark,
New Jersey. He married that Jane Barter whose uncle was
a partner in Chuck Full O'Nuts before he divorced her last
year after playing around, I think I gathered from you, with
some other woman, you-never-said-who. And, after all, he
didn't marry her either."

"Didn't he?" Mary said dully, choked with rage against
herself for having as much as mentioned Nathan to Sarah.

"When you came last March you told me he was after marrying Carrie Brindle, a rich Jewish girl from Buffalo. Surely you remember?"

Mary could only give a miserable little laugh.

"You told me about it last March! When you came off the *Liberté*. You told me," Sarah smiled lovingly and admiringly, "how he gave yourself orchids for your birthday in January."

"Why, and so he did!" Mary laughed gaily, her anger with herself mounting and spilling. Last March, coming off that damned six-days boat of loneliness, she had had to talk to somebody about him.

"He is a very handsome man," Sarah smiled gently. Mary stared at her. "You showed me his photograph."

"Did I really?" Mary gurgled, and spread her ringed fingers indifferently. "Richard and I meet so many people."

Sarah sighed.

"It must be grand to be getting orchids. That was the only time in my life I saw orchids." She laughed at her own ignorance. "I thought they were passion flowers. I forgot to ask you," with a happy smile, "was it Mr. Cash gave them to you before you sailed?"

Mary looked swiftly at her, but it was plain that she was not probing. Sarah's questions were always innocent, pointless, without guile. She looked out, frowningly, at the granite brown of the old North Gate, under whose arch the almost-silent Main Street of Ardagh flows into the completely silent countryside. She heard the soft *cric-croc* of a cart entering slowly under the arch from the farther side. The little cart slowly emerged from under the arch, salmon-pink, bearing its pyramid of black peat, drawn by a tiny, gray donkey. It *cric-crocked* slowly past her vision. She found herself murmuring as softly and slowly, feeling

as she did so that this was exactly how she had been
wheedled last March into talking about Nathan:

"I bought those orchids last March. I just had to have
them."

"Why, Mary?" — gently.

"I was feeling very down."

"What happened to you?" — sympathetically.

"I'd had a terrible quarrel with a friend."

"Who, Mary?" — tenderly.

"A friend. Nobody you know. A woman. A woman
called Gold. Nancy Gold. There was nobody to see me
off on the boat. Richard had gone by plane direct to Berne.
The cabin looked empty. No flowers. No bottle of champagne. No basket of fruit. When I went down to lunch I
stood at the turn of the staircase and saw all those men
and women chattering around all those white tables and
all the women wearing corsages. I turned back and went
up to the florist and I bought me two orchids."

Neither of them spoke for a while.

"Well, well," Sarah concluded. "And so he married the
Jewish woman in the heel of the hunt. Is he happy with
her, would you say?"

"How should I know? We never meet. I'm not sure that
I like him very much really."

Sarah smiled in loyal admiration.

"He liked you once, though. Enough anyway to give
you the orchids."

"That was just one night going to the opera. I thought
at the time it was a little plush of him. Still, a woman
likes those little attentions."

"You always liked nice things. You always liked those
little attentions. I can see why you bought them for yourself on the boat."

"It was just that I was down in the mouth."

"And then there was Richard on your mind, too."

"Richard?" Mary stared at her as if she was a witch or a fortuneteller.

"I mean you were worried about him."

"Was I?"

"He was ill. You left here after three days to be with him. I knew the minute you came in the door, Mary, off that old boat, that you weren't your old self."

Mary gave her a desperate look. She got up.

"I think I'll go for a stroll. I have a bit of a headache."

She went out, under the arch, so unmistakably a foreigner in her high-collared mink coat, her furry hat and her spiked heels that the few townsfolk who were in the Sunday street stared at her, but sideways so as not to be seen staring. She saw none of them, nothing, none of the familiar names over the shuttered shops, unchanged for as long as she could remember — Fenelon the grocer, Ryan the draper, Shorthall's Garage, Morgan and Corneille, Furnishers, Upholsterers and Undertakers, Saint Anne's Nursing Home and Dr. Freeman's brass plate polished into holes at the corners. The street petered out where a bright yellow signpost directed her across the bridge to the dark yellow furze on the rising foothills.

She leaned over the limestone parapet, lit a cigarette, and glared along the barely flowing river with its shallow autumn pools and its dry beaches. She pounded the parapet with her gloved fist and said, aloud: "It's intolerable!" Her cigarette ash floated down into the river. On one side of the river were the long gardens at the back of the Main Street's houses, coming right down to the riverbank; and, farther on, plumb with the river, the backs of old donkey-gray warehouses, decaying now, eyeless, little used since the river silted up and ceased to be navigable. The Franciscan belfry was reflected in an islanded pool among the gravel at the bend of the river, and in the pool a sweep of yellow from the far hills that rose to the farther mountains over whose rounded backs the sailing clouds had long ago seemed so often to call her to come away, to come away. Today the clouds were one solid, frozen mass, tomb-like, so that if they moved they moved massively, and she could not tell if they moved at all.

She had rowed across the river down there, that Mid-summer Eve, with Annie Grey, and Tommy Morgan, and Joe Fenelon and Molly Cardew. She had borrowed her daddy's Gramophone and twelve of his gayest Italian records, and halfway across, the records, which she had placed on top of the Gramophone, began to slide one by one into the water with gentle plops. Midsummer heat, and a great sky of stars and the whole of Ardagh sound asleep. While waiting for the sun to rise they swam in one of the pools, and then, at the first ghost of light, not light, a hint of morning, they lit the fire and played a muffled "O Sole Mio" and a wind blew the woodash into the cups of wine that Joe Fenelon had stolen from his father's shop. She had not thought of that gray dust in the wine for seventeen years. It was, she thought savagely, the sort of thing that Sarah's memories never remembered, along with the gaiety of Corney Canty, and the way redheaded Molly Cardew used to tickle the back of Tommy Morgan's neck so that he would hunch up his shoulders and say, affection-ately-irritably, "Go away, you green frog you!" and poor weak-minded Joe Fenelon's lovely tenor voice singing "I'll Take Ye Home Again, Kathleen" at every party. The ash in the wine was just another piece of her real life immured, with the bones of everything she had ever done or said, in the vaults of Sarah's infallible memoirs. Would Nathan Cash one day join these dead bones? Had he already

gone there, with all she had been through because of him?
Would all her life, unless she really went away and left her
past behind her?

She blew out a long breath of smoke and threw her cigarette into the river. She would call in to Shorthall's Garage
on the way home. The car would come for her at nine in
the morning. By evening she would be floating down over
the pinewoods on the little hills about the airstrip at
Zurich. Blonde hostesses. Pure-white washrooms. ("Just
like Newark," Richard had once laughed.) And her ritual
first cup of *café au lait* at the tall counter, while Richard
waited with Donna, and Biddy and Patrick. But she did
not stir until a soft rain began to fall, a dew, a mist, and she
was aware that it was dusk. The streets were empty, the
slates shone purple. The turf smoke medicinal in the air.
She stopped by the garage, passed on, stopped again,
hesitated again, half turned back and then, with a groan,
went on to the house. She went upstairs to her room and
lay there, with the last pallor of the day in the great mirror
of the wardrobe, until dinnertime.

For their coffee they sat in the bay window. They gos-
siped amiably, Mary half listening, her head half turned
to the footfalls passing down the street to evening Bene-
diction at the Franciscan priory. Sarah said:

"By the way, Mary, wasn't it very sad about your poor
friend, Mrs. Henry Beirne!"

Mary turned her head a little farther towards the window, as if she were trying to hear something out there,
but really to hide the look of blank fear that she could feel
coming into her eyes. She knew no Mrs. Henry Beirne. Her
frightened efforts to recall the woman produced nothing
clearer than the vague cloud that a drop of absinthe forms
in a glass of water, a fume like smoke, a wavering embryo

without a face. The last ghostly footstep faded. She whispered, groping for information:

"Yes. It was very sad. How did you know about it?"

"The Dublin papers had it on account of the other woman being related to the Bishop of Kilkenny. I don't think she could be more than thirty-two. Would you say so?"

"Surely more?" — groping still. Could it be a divorce? Or an accident? Why couldn't Sarah say what happened? Was the woman dead? The wraith in the water began to curl into another as yet undecipherable shape. She said gently: "Was her age given in the papers?"

"Not at all, but, sure, 'tis easy to work it out. We know she was the Class of Forty-one. Give her twenty or twenty-one at the Commencement, and wasn't it then she first met Henry Beirne? He proposed to her that very evening on the Common. You danced with him at the Ritz that night. You had the gold dress with the cream insets. How many children was it you said they had?"

As the white shape in the water took on a remembered face, Mary barely stopped herself from saying, "My God, it must be nine years since I saw that bitch Lucy Burbank." She said, dully:

"Children? Four" — and immediately regretted it, realizing that to say anything precise to Sarah about anything was only laying the ground for more questions next year, or in three or five years' time, when she would have completely forgotten what she had earlier said. They talked a little more about Lucy Burbank-Beirne, but Mary never did find out what exactly happened to her that was so very sad.

"It's time we lit the lamp," Sarah said.

It was dark. The rain had stopped and restarted. The footsteps had all returned the way they had come. In another hour the only sound in the long, winding street would be the drip of rain. Not a ground-floor window would be lit. There would not even be a Civic Guard out on a wet night like this. She gathered up the coffee cups and took them out to the kitchen on the old silver-plated salver, with the copper showing through, that her father had won at a golf tournament forty years ago. She returned and lifted off the pink globe of the oil lamp, her back to Sarah, and then lifted off the glass chimney, and put a match to the two charred wicks and watched the flame creep across their ridged edges. She replaced the glass chimney. Still with her back to Sarah, she said:

"I have bad news to break to you, Sarah."

"Oh, Mary, don't frighten me."

"I've been trying to get myself to tell you since I came."

"What is it, love?"

Carefully she replaced the pink globe, aware of its warm light under her chin.

"Richard has given up his job. I came alone this time. I came only to tell you. I must go away tomorrow morning."

She slowly raised the first wick, and then the second wick, and felt the room behind her fill with light. She heard a noise like a drip of rain, or melting snow, or oozing blood.

"Oh, Mary, don't go away from me!"

She turned. For the first time, Sarah was pleading with her, her little brown face smaller than ever under the great cloud of hair, her two brown spaniel's eyes brimming with tears.

"I must go!" Mary cried, her two fists trembling by her side. "I must go!"

"I'll never see you again!"

Mary sank on her knees and looped her arms lovingly about her waist.

"Of course you will, you silly-billy," she laughed. "You'll see me lots of times."

They gazed at one another fondly for a long while. Then Mary rose and went to the dark window and drew the curtains together with a swish. Arranging the folds of the curtains, she said, reassuringly, like a mother to a child:

"You'll see me lots of times. Lots and lots of times."

Behind her, Sarah said resignedly:

"Will I, Mary?"

The Sugawn Chair

Every autumn I am reminded of an abandoned sugawn chair that languished for years, without a seat, in the attic of my old home. It is associated in my mind with an enormous sack which the carter used to dump with a thud on the kitchen floor around every October. I was a small kid then, and it was as high as myself. This sack had come "up from the country," a sort of diplomatic messenger from the fields to the city. It smelled of dust and hay and apples, for the top half of it always bulged with potatoes, and, under a layer of hay, the bottom half bulged with apples. Its arrival always gave my mother great joy and a little sorrow, because it came from the farm where she had been born. Immediately she saw it she glowed with pride in having a "back," as she called it — meaning something behind her more solid and permanent than city streets, though she was also saddened by the memories that choked her with this smell of hay and potatoes from the home farm, and apples from the little orchard near the farmhouse. My father, who had also been born on a farm, also took great pleasure in these country fruits, and as the two of them stood over the sack, in the kitchen, in the middle of the humming city, everything that their youth had meant to them used to make them smile and laugh and use words that they had never used during the rest of the year, and which I thought magical: words like *late sowing, clover crop, inch field, marl bottom, headlands, tubers,* and the names of potatoes, British Queens or Arran Banners, that sounded to me like the names of regiments. For those moments my father and mother became a young, courting couple again. As they stood over that sack, as you might say warming their hands to it, they were intensely happy, close to each other, in love again. To me they were two very old people. Counting back now, I reckon that they were about forty-two or forty-three.

One autumn evening after the sack arrived, my father went up to the attic and brought down the old sugawn chair. I suppose he had had it sent up from his home farm. It was the only thing of its kind in our house, which they had filled — in the usual peasants' idea of what constitutes elegance — with plush chairs, gold-framed pictures of Stags at Bay, and exotic tropical birds, pelmets on the mantelpieces, Delft shepherdesses, Chinese mandarins with nodding heads, brass bedsteads with mighty knobs and mother-of-pearl escutcheons set with bits of mirror, vast mahogany chiffoniers, and so on. But the plush-bottomed chairs, with their turned legs and their stiff backs, were for show, not for comfort, whereas in the old country sugawn chair my da could tilt and squeak and rock to his behind's content.

It had been in the place for years, rockety, bockety, chipped and well-polished, and known simply as "your father's chair," until the night when, as he was reading the *Evening Echo* with his legs up on the kitchen range, there was a sudden rending noise, and down he went through the seat of it. There he was then, bending over, with the chair stuck onto him, and my mother and myself in the splits of laughter, pulling it from him while he cursed like a trooper. This was the wreck that he now suddenly brought down from the dusty attic.

The next day, he brought in a great sack of straw from

the Cornmarket, a half-gallon of porter and two old bud-
dies from the street — an ex-soldier known to the kids
around as "Tear-'em-and-ate-'em" and a little dwarf of a
man who guarded the stage door at the Opera House when
he was not being the sacristan at the chapel. I was enchanted when I heard what they were going to do. They
were going to make ropes of straw — a miracle I had never
heard of — and reseat the chair. Bursting with pride in
my da, I ran out and brought in my best pal, and the two
of us sat as quiet as cats on the kitchen table, watching the
three men filling the place with dust, straw, and loud arguments as they began to twist the ropes for the bottom of the
chair.

More strange words began to float in the air with the
dust: *scallops, flat tops, bulrushes, cipeens, fields in great
heart* . . . And when the three sat down for a swig of
porter, and looked at the old polished skeleton in the middle of the floor, they began to rub the insides of their
thighs and say how there was no life at all like the country life, and my mother poured out more porter for them,
and laughed happily when my da began to talk about
horses, and harrows, and a day after the plow, and how,
for *that* much, he'd throw up this blooming city life altogether and settle down on a bit of a farm for the heel of
his days.

This was a game of which he, she and I never got tired,
a fairy tale that was so alluring it did not matter a damn
that they had not enough money to buy a window box, let
alone a farm of land.

"Do you remember that little place," she would say,
"that was going last year down at Nantenan?"

When she said that, I could see the little reedy fields of
Limerick that I knew from holidays with my uncle, and the
crumbling stone walls of old demesnes with the moss and

saffron lichen on them, and the willow sighing softly by the Deel, and I could smell the wet turf rising in the damp air, and, above all, the tall wildflowers of the mallow, at first cabbage-leaved, then pink and coarse, then gossamery, then breaking into cakes that I used to eat — a rank weed that is the mark of ruin in so many Irish villages, and whose profusion and color is for me the sublime emblem of Limerick's loneliness, loveliness and decay.

"Ah!" my da would roar. "You and your blooming ould Limerick! That bog of a place! Oh, but, God blast it, why didn't I grab that little farm I was looking at two years ago there below Emo!"

"Oho, ho, ho!" she would scoff. "The Queen's! The Lousy Queen's! God, I'd live like a tiger and die like a Turk for Limerick. For one patch of good old Limerick. Oh, Limerick, my love, and it isn't alike! Where would you get spuds and apples the like of them in the length and breadth of the Queen's County?"

And she grabbed a fist of hay from the bag and buried her face in it, and the tears began to stream down her face, and me and my pal screaming with laughter at her, and the sacristan lauding Tipperary, and the voices rose as Tear-'em-and-ate-'em brought up the River Barrow and the fields of Carlow, until my da jumped up with:

"Come on, lads, the day is dyin' and acres wide before us!"

For all that, the straw rope was slow in emerging. Their arguments about it got louder and their voices sharper. At first all their worry had been whether the kitchen was long enough for the rope; but so far, only a few, brief worms of straw lay on the red tiles. The sacristan said: "That bloody straw is too moist." When he was a boy in Tipp he never seen straw the like o' that. Tear-'em-and-ate-'em said that straw was old straw. When he was a lad in Carlow they

never used old straw. Never! Under no possible circumstances! My dad said: "What's wrong with that straw is it's
too bloomin' short!" And they began to kick the bits with
their toes, and grimace at the heap on the floor, and pick
up bits and fray them apart and throw them aside until
the whole floor was like a stable. At last they put on their
coats, and gave the straw a final few kicks, and my pal
jumped down and said he was going back to his handball
and, in my heart, I knew that they were three impostors.

The kitchen was tidy that evening when I came back
with the *Evening Echo*. My da was standing by the sack of
potatoes. He had a spud in his fist, rubbing off the dust of
its clay with his thumb. When he saw me he tossed it back
in the sack, took the paper, took one of the plush-bottom
chairs and sat on it with a little grimace. I did not say anything, but young as I was, I could see that he was not
reading what he was looking at. God knows what he was
seeing at that moment.

For years the anatomy of the chair stood in one of the
empty attics. It was there for many years after my father
died. When my mother died and I had to sell out the few
bits of junk that still remained from their lives, the dealer
would not bother to take the useless frame, so that when,
for the last time, I walked about the echoing house, I found
it standing alone in the middle of the bare attic. As I
looked at it I smelled apples, and the musk of Limerick's
dust, and the turf-tang from its cottages, and the mallows
among the limestone ruins, and I saw my mother and my
father again as they were that morning — standing over
the autumn sack, their arms about one another, laughing
foolishly, and madly in love again.

A Shadow,
Silent as a Cloud

In the empty dining room, lit by a single electric bulb hanging from the rosette in the ceiling, the black-marble clock chimed slowly seven times and a sputter of rain tapped at the windows. The three tables, long, white and narrow, arranged like the letter U, looked very white under that single bulb. At one end of the top table there was a waitress, moving slowly from chair to chair, looking at the cards bearing the names of the guests she would have to serve. She was about fifty, but still handsome and well-shaped though a bit on the dumpy side. She murmured the names in different voices to suit her notion of what they might look like. She said *Miss Olive Harold* in a thin-lipped and prim voice. It was a Protestant sort of name, a hard-faced name. She made *Mr. Condon Larkin* into a soft, round-faced man. She said *Miss Stella Shannon* twice, it was such a nice name, young, and lovely, and a bit lost. *Mr. Kevin Lowry* could be a gloomy sort of fellow, or he could be a jolly, laughing fellow. *Monsignor O'Connell* . . . A bit of wood ash fell from the fire, which was quietly oozing wet sap. She made a crooked mouth at the initials of *Professor J. T. G. Quigley's* name. The next card was at the center of the table, the chairman's place. *Jeremiah J. Collis.*

She looked over at the fire and saw a gate lodge with a thick laurel copse around it, almost a quarter-acre of close-planted laurels, trimmed level at about four feet from the ground, a miniature forest into which she used to crawl on the crinkling brown leaves. There was a bay tree. She looked up across the wide, spreading pasture to the white door pillars of the Big House. Behind it there were the rolling mountains. On quiet days you could hear the tramcars at Rathfarnham village jolting over the junction points. Her lips, without speaking it, shaped the single word, *Templeogue*. She did not notice that the piece of fallen wood was giving out a pungent smell, like laurel burning. She was still there, with one hand on the chair back, smiling at the fire, when the headwaiter came in and switched on all the lights, and then all the other waiters and hired waitresses like herself came in after him in a chattering gaggle. The headwaiter directed them to their stations, and there they stood, as straight as statues, until the first group of guests came hesitantly to the big doorway and began to cluster around the seating plan on the easel beside it.

She recognized him immediately he came in. He was after getting terribly loguey; his hair was gray at the sides; his chin bulged over his white tie; but he was a fine figure of a man still. He passed to his place, talking and laughing with a soft, pretty young woman with coils of fair hair on top of her head. She had a pale face, red lips and a wrinkled forehead. He called her Stella and it was as plain as a pikestaff that he was gone about her. When he sat down she saw the thin patch on top of his head, but when he said over his shoulder, "The wine list, please," she thought his voice was just the same voice, only grown older. When she got the wine list and put it into his backward-stretching hand, the professor beside him was saying, "All right, Jerry, but I warn you that if you don't phrase it very carefully they will misunderstand your motives." At that he laughed, and his laugh was a boy's laugh.

From that on she was much too busy to look at him again, until he got up to give the toast of "Ireland," and said, "You may smoke, gentlemen." After a while he laid down his cigar and tapped his coffee cup with his spoon, and stood up to give his speech. She moved over by the left-hand table to take a good stock of him. His vest had burst its bottom button, his jowls were flushed from the wine and the heat, but still and all he really was a fine figure of a man.

During the first few minutes she did not take in one word he said, she felt so nervous for him, but she soon became aware that he was entirely at his ease and she started to listen with interest.

"And so, I hope you can now see, ladies and gentlemen, why I have called my address by the slightly sentimental title 'Lest We Forget.' Because it does seem to me that we architects forget far too much and far too easily in our eagerness to invent, to innovate, to be modern and progressive. Instead, my feeling is that we should encourage our memories to interrupt us in our haste, to pursue us as we run away from them, to surprise and halt us by the richness of the message that the past can lay in our hands, warning us to go easy when we are going too fast and too far. After all, when you come to think of it, what else is memory but the recognition of experience? And" — he held out his hands appealingly and smiled around the tables — "let's be honest, what else, all too often, is this famous experience of ours — about which we are always boasting to our juniors — what else is it but the lamentable record of our carefully concealed mistakes?"

For that he got a little laughter and ironic applause.

"Now, I don't pretend to any special wisdom, and I am not yet quite as old as the Methuselah of George Bernard Shaw, or," with a deferential little bow and a smile towards the Monsignor, "should I have said the Methuselah of that somewhat more famous author, Genesis?"

They all craned to look at the Monsignor. Seeing him smile indulgently, they crackled into a light laughter. At the next sentence she saw, with amusement, the wry way he touched his thin poll.

"Yet even I sometimes become aware of mortal dissolution and feel the falling of the leaves."

The words and the gesture evoked more laughter. As if he knew that he had their full attention now he leaned forward on his ten finger tips and let his voice become warm and serious.

"Perhaps that is why I feel so certain that I know what we are all afraid of? We are afraid of being thought old-fashioned. And yet can there be any single one of us, whether young or old, who will dare to deny that our profession is as much concerned with the passing away of old things as with their replacement by new things? That we have something to learn from the very things that we are destroying? For is it not true that to create is in some sense to change, and to change is in some sense to destroy? All creative work is a form of destruction."

He leaned up and held a longer pause of silence than he had dared before, and, for a while after, he spoke quite conversationally, almost carelessly:

"It's very hard, whenever I drive out of Dublin, not to feel a bit sorry when I look around me at the ranks of new and shining houses stretching out and out all around the old battered center I've left behind me. I naturally feel a sense of professional pride in these new homes, but I feel sad because those new settlements — it is the only word for them — have no tradition, no feel of the past, no memories, and they have been built on fields that, for generations upon generations, were full of associations and memories.

In all these building schemes of ours let us never forget that we are bartering something that is as eloquent as it is old for something that, however good and necessary, is as mute and dumb as it is unappeasably strange and new."

She paused briefly, and in that moment she heard the young man at her elbow whispering across the table to another young man: "Clever bastard! Here comes the Templeogue job." Alerted and annoyed, she began to listen more carefully. He was still speaking quite easily, without any flourish of any kind, voice or hands:

"It would be insulting to this Institute of ours to suggest for a moment that anybody here thinks that architecture is just so much mute stone. Every city is the richer for having absorbed something of the vibrations of the living and the dead. It is not merely that we like to know that somebody famous spoke from this loggia or died on those steps; that in our own capital such noble spirits as Edmund Burke, or Oliver Goldsmith, or Tom Moore, or Charles Stewart Parnell, or Patrick Pearse walked these streets or died within the sounds of their traffic — it makes architecture more living that countless humble citizens have hollowed the steps of a church or sat in the benches of some old school. Must we always barter away that livingness of the dead for the weaker pulsations and meaner associations of the passing day?"

With that one passionate question he picked up and tossed away his card of jottings. Then he smiled and was casual again:

"You know, you could evoke a whole century with one glance at Sheridan the playwright's house in Dorset Street. But I challenge even the most pugnacious gentleman among ye to say that he feels his dander rise today as he changes gear among the red-roofed bungalows of modern Donnybrook."

He let the ripple of chuckles die away. As he went on she thought he threw a glance at Miss Shannon.

"Or could even the youngest and most romantic lady present confess that she ever thinks of poor Pamela, Lord Edward's unhappy widow, as she whirls in the number eight bus past the Frascati of modern Blackrock? It is the same everywhere. It is right and proper to build new homes. Do we have to do it by knocking down the bridges of history?"

At this, the young man near her who had whispered across the table leaned back in his chair and sighed audibly at the ceiling.

"Yet even in my boyhood places like Rathfarnham were still the haunts of wandering tinkers, wild birds and strolling lovers. The rural charm of Templeogue still had that air of seclusion which once drew Charles Lever and his young bride to live and love there among the fields and hedgerows, within view of the rolling drums of the Dublin mountains topped by the Hell Fire Club and the cairns of the Three Rock. Must this too, this latest place to be threatened by what we grandiosely call Urban Development, also be utterly destroyed? Must we lose entirely the inheritance of our Irish past?"

The earnestness of this sentence won him a clatter of applause. Even she joined in, and all the louder because the contemptuous young man in front of her was now groaning in audible pain into his two fists. Jerry was now racing on eloquently, but she no longer heard him. With bright, moist eyes she saw only the old gate lodge, the laurel copse, the motionless swing hanging from the beech, and under it the oily celandines and the yellow aconites. Besides, her eyes had wandered to Miss Shannon and Mr. Condon Larkin. Miss Shannon's left hand hung down by the side of her chair, Mr. Larkin's right hand hung by the

side of his, and the two hands gently fondled one another.
She was leaning forward, chin on elbowed palm; he was
leaning back; both were looking up at the speaker. Anyone
could tell that they were not paying the slightest attention
to his words.

By the time she had done her part in clearing the tables
the bar was packed out, but she saw him, taller than all the
rest, in the middle of the crush, arguing with Miss Shannon,
Mr. Condon Larkin, Professor Quigley, and two or three
of the younger men, including the contemptuous young
man, who had, she now saw, a beaky nose, tousled fair hair
and a slight tuft of fair beard, two prominent teeth and
fierce, small blue eyes. He was very angry, and as she
pushed nearer she heard him saying in a voice loud enough
to be heard above the general babble:

"It's all a damned lot of sentimentality. And I don't
believe you mean a bloody word of it. And as for dragging
in Tommy Moore, may God forgive you! Now, Edmund
Burke I'll grant ye! Dammit, I'll even give you Parnell!
But, God Almighty, not Tommy Moore!"

Jerry was also angry.

"And what," he demanded from the heights, "what, pray,
is wrong with Tom Moore?"

The professor looked as if he was trying to calm them
both. The toothy young man spat back in an insulting
voice:

"He was a sentimentalist, and wurrse than a sentimentalist. He was a calculating sentimentalist. That thing on his
sleeve . . . What was it but the price ticket of a turn-
coat?"

"Now, now," the professor intervened, "it was a heart all
the same. A song like 'Oft in the Stilly Night' could not
have been composed by a man without real feeling."

"Feeling! To conceal what? Ambition! Like all senti-mentalists he . . ."

The professor shot a frightened look around the bar — they were all talking at the tops of their voices — and laid a hand on the young man's shoulder, saying:

"Nevertheless, Mr. Collyer, it is a lovely song. Jerry, raise it for us. Give us a bar."

"I will, then," Jerry said. She withdrew as he laid his glass on the counter, crying, "And if I maul it itself it'll still be a fine song. Silence for your president!" he shouted, and although a few of them gave a mock-serious cheer, gradually the whole bar fell silent. He cleared his throat and began to sing with feeling. As she stood by the door, half in the corridor, listening, others came along from the lounge to listen. She thought it was splendid the way he put his heart into it, in his fine, deep bass voice, especially when he came to the low, vibrating notes of:

> *The smiles, the tears of boyhood years,*
> *The words of love then spoken . . .*

He was looking all the time at Stella Shannon, who kept looking from under her worried brows at Condon Larkin, whose eyes kept expanding and contracting nervously in an evident effort to keep sober.

When the clapping ended, Jerry took back his glass with a sweep and winked triumphantly at young Collyer. Before they could resume their argument she sent in the Boots to him. She watched the Boots touch his arm and whisper, and Jerry look out at her over the heads of the crowd. He came towards her, turning to wag a smug finger at the young man, crying, "When I've squared up for the wine I'll be back. I won't let you get away with it as easily as all that, my young boyo!" He was groping in his tails for his wallet as he crushed through the door out to her. She moved a few feet up the corridor away from the bar and the noise.

"The wine?" he said. "How much?"

"It's not the wine, Jerry." She smiled when he opened his eyes haughtily at her use of his first name. "I see you don't remember me?"

"I'm very sorry," he apologized. "I gather I ought to remember you. But as a matter of fact I just don't."

She laughed and felt herself blushing.

"You once asked me to marry you. I was twelve at the time. My name is Lily Collis now but I used to be Lily Braden when you knew me long ago. I married a cousin of your own — Victor Collis. He was Uncle Mel's son. We used all be playing together by Uncle Mel's lodge at Templeogue. Do you forget?"

He saw a red plush divan beside him.

"Won't you sit down?" he said to her gently.

"Ah, no, it wouldn't be right, I should really be in the lounge now, I'm on duty there, and at the dance afterwards. Am I embarrassing you?"

"Good Lord, no, not in the least. But I am going to sit down."

He sat, and looked up at her and laughed.

"You used to have long fair plaits of hair down your back. I was gone about you. I used to swing you on the old beech tree. Twenty swings for a kiss. Wasn't that the tariff?" She laughed happily. "So you married Uncle Mel's boy. There were such a lot of Collises. From Glasnevin, the North Circular Road, Howth, Raheny, and a few on the south side at Cabinteely, and old Templeogue. Do you realize, Lily, that it must be nearly thirty years since I last laid eyes on you?"

"It is, and thirty-seven years ago. I was thirteen when

we last saw one another and you were sixteen. You're every bit of fifty-three, Jerry."

He raised mock-pleading palms, laughing again.

"Spare my last remaining gray hairs."

"I simply had to speak to you when I heard you talking about the old place tonight. It's marvelous the way you remember it so well. The path through the wood, and the pond behind the lodge, and the old swing and all."

"And the smell of the wood-smoke," he said.

"And the geese pickin' in the grass."

"And the old avenue all weeds," he laughed.

"And the old stables falling down," she cried.

"Do you remember the day the hunt chased a fox across the avenue?"

"I see you have it all!" she cried.

They were silent, looking at one another. In the bar a woman's voice had begun to sing "Has Sorrow Thy Young Days Shaded?"

"They're still at it about Tom Moore," he said.

In a mirror facing into the bar she saw that the singer was Miss Shannon.

"Uncle Mel!" Jerry was saying, staring up at her. "He ran away to sea when he was a boy, and came back, and married into the gate lodge. He had a four-master in a bottle in the fanlight."

"You know that he killed himself in the heel of the hunt?"

"Ah, no! For God's sake!"

"He was left alone in the lodge after Victor married me. One winter he got raging pneumonia and he wouldn't give in to it. They picked him up one night off the steps of the Parnell monument and took him across to the Rotunda hospital. He'd tell nobody who he was or where he lived, so they took him up to the Workhouse and he died there. It was only after he was buried, in the paupers' graveyard, that we heard about it. I think it was a sort of wild revenge he took on Victor for marrying me. But the Collises were always like that — wild and obstinate and vengeful."

He shook his head, half sadly, half proudly.

"God knows, Lily, and that's a true bill. Do you know that I didn't speak to my father for seven years before he died? And all over nothing but politics. I pushed myself through college under my own steam. When he was gone I had to support my mother and my two sisters. I climbed to the top of the tree with my two bare hands. But, by God, I did it. Nothing stopped me and nothing ever will stop me from getting what I want. Oho! We're an obstinate set all right. Tell me, what happened at all to Uncle Ned Collis?"

She threw her head sideways to laugh again, but this time her laugh was a half groan.

"There was a wild divil o' hell for you. Always hitting the bottle. Once when he was on a batter didn't he lose his ship at the North Wall, and what did he do but dive into the Liffey and swim after it to the Poolbeg light-house, where he knew it would be halting. He died raving in New Orleans."

He had once been in New Orleans. He saw the mists and the lights on the Mississippi. His eyes blazed:

"Divils o' hell, every one of them! My mother often told me about a Collis woman who swam from Ireland's Eye to the Bailey lighthouse around by Balscadden, a swim no man ever did before or since." He got up and took her hand in his two hands. "Lily, there's nobody like the old stock. There was always great stuff in us." He felt her ring, looked at it and back at her. "Family?"

"Three, two boys and a girl. Not that they're boys any longer. The eldest is married. He went off to England last month. He's a doctor. The second is on a ship; he's a radio officer. Annie's at home; she's a radiologist." She paused, saw him look over her uniform, smiled proudly. "You know Victor well — he's the headwaiter at the Oyster."

"Good Lord, I must have seen him every week of my life for the last ten years. Why didn't he talk to me and say who he was?"

"It wouldn't be right. But leave you talk to him the next time you go into the Oyster."

"I will."

But he had the premonition that he would never dine at the Oyster again. She went on:

"Now that the children are grown up I take a relief job like this now and again. For a night, for a week. What do I want sitting at home in Ringsend doing nothing? I'm here just for tonight. Tomorrow, now, I'll go around and see the lakes."

"So you married and lived happy ever afterwards."

"Since you wouldn't have me," she laughed coyly. "But what about yourself?"

He released her hand.

"I'm an old dyed-in-the-wool bachelor, Lily. I was too busy and ambitious for that sort of thing when I was young, and now that I'm an old codger nobody wants me."

"Nonsense, Jerry," she said maternally. "I saw you throwing great sheep's eyes at Miss Shannon. You'll get married one of these days. But I'm keeping you from your friends, and I ought to be on the job. It was grand talking about old times, Jerry. I'm glad one Collis anyway made a success of his life. You gave a great speech. They're all talking about it in the lounge. They say you're sure to be given the job. What is it?"

He made a little grimace.

"Just a big housing scheme. But all I'm interested in is

that whoever gets it should do it properly. Old things are precious, Lily. The older I grow the more I feel it."

"Of course you should get it," she declared loyally. "Who better? And I hope you'll make a packet of money out of it."

They shook hands warmly. He watched her walking away from him down the corridor. A tidy figure. Handsome. Full of courage. And damned intelligent. In the bar Stella's song was dying sweetly and sadly.

> *If thus the cold world now wither*
> *Each feeling that once was dear* . . .

He hesitated, saw a French window beside him, opened it and stepped out into the night.

The darkness was moist but warm. The whole sky one basketful of stars. Feeling a gravel path under his shoes, he walked slowly along it until he heard the lake lapping the shore like a cat, and, as he grew accustomed to the dark, he made out a small wooden wharf jutting into the waves in the lee of a boathouse. He smelled laurels, and rotting wrack and reeds. He leaned against the shed, and half saw the wide lakes stretching all around, with their black islands, and their peaked mountains cutting off the stars. The south wind flowed gently and indifferently over it all.

Afterwards he would say, "She gave me a bit of a shake, I can tell you." Yet what it was in their brief encounter that disturbed him he could never say. All he knew was that he had felt a shadow, silent as a cloud, that he had not heeded for many years, and a sudden wish to be alone with it. He stayed by the lake for the length of three cigarettes.

They had lived recklessly, some of them wildly, all of them devil-may-cares who took life in both hands and squandered it without calculation. But because they had lived like that they did not need pity. Old Ned, diving drunk off the side of the quay and swimming after his ship? He'd have spat on pity! "Died raving in New Orleans . . ." They had refused, rejected, despised something precious, and powerful and real, but they were not failures. Failures were another kind of drunk altogether, fellows like Condon Larkin, hanging around waiting for some-body's pity to pick them out of the gutter. He whipped his second cigarette out of his case and lit it with an angry click of his lighter. Failures are ambitious, calculating peo-ple, men who feel disaster in the softest wind. It was not that they were just reckless. Lily was a Collis. With her eyes that could skiver you, and her hard little body like a pony, and her hands like plates, and her three children she'd slaved for, made one a doctor, one a radiologist, sent one to sea, as she sent old Victor padding off every morn-ing and evening to the Oyster in his black tie and his tails. He saw their box of a house in Ringsend, red brick, three windows, a green door with an iron knocker, one of hun-dreds like it, near the sooty church by the canal basin, never free of the rattle of the trams, car lights flashing across the ceilings, ships' sirens on the Liffey. He laughed admiringly. Just the sort of woman who would have swum from Ireland's Eye to the Bailey lighthouse and back again. With a gasp of anger he flicked his cigarette in a red arc into the water. "She knocked me off my stilts somehow," he would say afterwards. But he would never admit that she had left him with a sense of smallness and shame.

Lighting his third cigarette, he turned in the direction of the hotel and the faint throb of dance music. Young Collyer would probably say that he was slobbering now about the small homes of the living as before about the big houses of the dead. He went on slowly beside a stony piece of beach and the slopping water until he saw to his left the bright windows beaming light down over the lawn to a white garden seat at the edge of the lake. One window was open. Through it he could see the dancers when they moved past it.

Halted, he was looking irresolutely at the window when he heard his name called from somewhere nearby. He made out a rustic summer house with a conical, thatched roof, at the end of a tiny side path. He walked towards it, peered in, and saw two cigarettes glowing in the dark.

"Who's there?" he asked.

"Us," said Stella's voice, softly.

He flicked on his cigarette lighter and held it like a torch over his head.

"The Statue of Liberty?" Stella's voice asked.

He made out Condon Larkin sitting beside her. Her shoulders were bare, her face pale, her neck as straight as a swan's, and he thought that she was looking at him quizzically. Just before he put out the flame he saw on the table between them a bottle of brandy. He stopped and entered and sat beside her, and, gradually, by the reflected sheen of the lights and the stars, he saw her better, and that her two hands were clasping a brandy glass as if it were a chalice. He felt a great knot of anger against Larkin bulging in his chest but he managed to say quietly:

"Stella, dear, don't you think it would be more prudent for you to sit indoors? Or at least to wear a wrap?"

Her head swayed feebly on her long neck like a daffodil in a slight wind, and she said in a kind parody of his voice:

"Dear Jerry. Prudent Jerry. Surely you ought to be indoors promoting your cause?"

Larkin leaned across her towards him and began to speak in the overslow, overcareful enunciation of all drunks.

"Mis-ter Pres-i-dent, we were discuss-ing you. I want to con-grat-ulate you, most sincerely. On a very subtle speech. Especially that part of your speech that dealt with Temple-ogue. I sincere-ly hope they will put you in charge of the entire scheme. I sincerely mean that."

"Shut up, Larkin," he said crossly.

"Stella! Our Pres-i-dent tells me to shut up. But I won't shut up. Why should I shut up? It was a very fine speech. And I repeat that."

"All right, Larkin! What you are trying to say, only you haven't the guts to say it straight out, is that all I care about is getting the Templeogue job. Thank you kindly."

Stella laid her hand on his, softly.

"Jerry! Condy and I have often talked about this. We believe that what you said about creating and destroying being very close to one another is true. Terribly true."

He realized from her touch and her tone that they were not mocking him: they really had liked his speech. Larkin leaned over again, crushing Stella against him in a blended waft of jasmine and brandy.

"She's right. It's terribly true! 'To create,' you said, 'is to change. And to change is to de-stroy.' And why is it true? It's true because every man who creates is a god-damned, flame-ing, bloody ego-tist. That's why I'll always be a dud. No, Stella!" he snarled querulously, shoving her hand away from him. "You've rubbed it into me often enough. I'm too diffident. I've no ambition. I'm a dud!"

She sighed at Jerry.

"It's why Condy and I liked your speech so much, Jerry. We feel that everybody should be more diffident. Let things grow naturally, like leaves. You know — the lilies of the field and all that. Condy says why should anybody impose his hand on the handiwork of God?"

His anger burst from him.

"But that isn't what I meant at all. We have to create whether we like it or not. People have to live in houses. We have to build for them, and go on building, even if it's only a road, a bridge, a culvert over a stream. We have to go on into the future. What I'd like to do is to maneuver vast schemes for living people about these old towns and villages, spread on and on and out and out, like an army of tanks sweeping in wide arcs about some country they want to conquer. We have to do it. Even if we don't want to do it life will make us do it, shoving us on behind. We can't help it!"

Larkin started to say something, and then gave up the ghost, his head sinking into his arms, his glass rolling over to the ground. Almost at once his heavy breathing showed that he had fallen asleep. For a moment Stella's hand hovered towards his head, and then slowly returned to her glass. She whispered:

"I'm afraid he's a weak argument against you. Actually he is a very good architect. He just hasn't got your drive."

He said irritably:

"This gazebo is as damp as a fungus. Let's get out of here for a minute for a breath of clean air."

She rose, and teetered a little. When he held her arm to steady her it was like taking a bird by the wing. Outside she lifted her furrowed forehead to the sky and murmured, "The stars of heaven." She had a strangely worn face for so young a woman. The pose had tautened her small breasts. He wanted to touch her bare shoulders.

"Stella! You'll never be able to do anything with him. He's not a good architect. He's not a good anything. He's just a drunk."

Still upward-looking, she waved a hand in weak deprecation.

"Please, don't bring all that up again."

"Stella! Is the real reason why you won't have me that I'm too old?"

She did not so much shake her head as let it roll from side to side, and then it rolled downward of its own weight so that she was looking out under her wrinkled forehead to where the light from the hotel touched the water's edge. He asked passionately:

"Why must you always go around picking people up out of the gutter? Lame dogs. Weaklings. Fellows who . . ."

She silenced him with a hand on his arm, and a backward look at the summer hut.

"Poor Condy!" she protested softly.

"And why not poor Jerry? Don't I deserve anything? Haven't I worked for it? Don't I deserve a wife, and a home, and children?"

"Poor Jerry," she placated with an appealing smile. "I'm sure you deserve a lot of things."

"But not from you?"

"I wouldn't be any use to you, Jerry. I'd always want to be whatever I am, and you would always be wanting to change me. Oh, I know you'd be kind to me, proud of me, preserve one little corner of me to show your friends, but you'd surround me, encircle me, swallow me up the way you would like to swallow up Templeogue."

They were silent for a moment, both looking out at the dark lake that slopped endlessly.

"So you really didn't believe a word I said tonight?"

"I believed it. But you did not. You are very ambitious, aren't you, Jerry?"

He did not answer her. He became so excited by the hope that she was asking a question about whose answer she was still in doubt that his fists in his pockets began to tremble, and he was made almost drunk by the scent of her body beside him, and the smells of the lake and the shore and the whispering waves. He did not look at her, but he knew that she was swaying gently by his side, looking up at him.

"All I want is you. You'd be my inspiration in everything I did."

"What a role!"

"I want nothing in the world but you."

"Not even Templeogue?"

"If I give up Templeogue will you marry me?"

"Yes! Like a shot!"

He said nothing. She lifted her head to the stars and began to laugh mockingly. She stopped suddenly. From inside the hut the sleepy voice groaned her name. She turned and faced the dark opening. She laid a hand on Jerry's arm.

"He's not a bad architect. He should have a job in the Board of Works, looking after old Georgian houses, old churches, old monuments. He has great taste, great reverence. There is a job vacant in the Board of Works. It would suit him perfectly. Could you say a word for him there, Jerry?"

He looked down at her delicate, worried, tiny face.

"Supposing I took that job myself, would you marry me?"

She shook her head drunkenly.

"Jerry! You might as well try to walk on the lake. We are what we are."

He took her forcibly by her bare shoulders.

"Stella! Stay with me, come away with me."

She released herself gently, went into the hut and composedly sat down. He saw her hand stroke the tousled head

on the table, and he knew in that instant that in trying to
save Larkin she would ruin her own life, and all sorts of
ideas jumbled wildly into him, such as that there is no such
thing as saving your life or squandering your life because
nobody knows what life is until he has lived out so much
of it that it is too late then to do anything but go on the way
you have gone on, or been driven on, from the beginning.
We are free to be, to act, to live, to create, to imagine, call
it whatever you like, only inside our own destiny, or else
to spit in the face of destiny and be destroyed by it. If a
man won't do that all he can do is to bake his bread and
throw it on the waters, and hope to God that what he is
doing — he gazed up and around him — is the will of the
night, the stars, the god of this whole flaming bloody un-
intelligible universe.

He turned and strode towards the lighted windows. The
central window of the middle three was a French window,
opening onto steps leading to the lawn. He went up there,
and stood in the opening, his hands in his pockets, his
shoulders back, watching the couples floating by, smiling
benevolently whenever his eye caught somebody he knew.
Presently he saw, on a settee in a corner, young Collyer
and Kevin Lowry with two young women. He advanced
towards them jauntily, swaying his shoulders and his tails,
beaming at them.

"Well, now!" he laughed, sitting between the two young
women and putting his arms around their shoulders. "Boys,
I see, will be boyos, and it follows that girls will be girlos!
Here, what are we drinking? Where are the bloody waiters?"

He raised an arm, clicked his fingers, and Lily Collis
came forward smiling. He winked at her.

"Tell the wine waiter to bring me two bottles of fizz,
Lily. The best in the house."

She cast a quick eye at the two young women, smiled at him and went off.

He had already turned eagerly to the young men, talking to them rapidly and forcefully. Between them was a low table with a white marble top. From his vest pocket he produced a gold pencil and with vigorous strokes he slashed lines across it to mark roads, avenues, fields, houses. At first they listened to him quizzically, giving one another long impassive looks, but by degrees his energy and his enthusiasm flooded them into the net of the discussion, so that when the champagne came they ignored it, leaning absorbedly over the table, pointing, arguing, laughing excitedly. The dancers floated by, the music drummed. Once he leaned back and glanced through the French window. The stars glinted. The dark lake lapped the shore.

A Touch of Autumn
in the Air

It was, of all people, Daniel Cashen of Roscommon who first made me realize that the fragments of any experience that remain in a man's memory, like bits and scraps of a ruined temple, are preserved from time not at random but by the inmost desires of his personality.

Cashen was neither sensitive nor intelligent. He was a caricature of the self-made, self-educated, nineteenth-century businessman. Some seventy years ago he had set up a small woolen factory in County Roscommon which, by hard work from early morning to late at night, and by making everybody around him work at the same pace, he developed into a thriving industry which he personally owned. His Swansdown Blankets, for example, were the only kind of blankets my mother ever bought. Though old when I made his acquaintance, he was still a powerful horse of a man, always dressed in well-pressed Irish tweeds, heavy countryman's boots, and a fawn, flat-topped bowler hat set squat above a big, red, square face, heavy handle-bar mustaches and pale blue, staring eyes of which one always saw the complete circle of the iris, challenging, concentrated, slightly mad.

One would not expect such a man to say anything very profound about the workings of the memory, and he did not. All he did was to indulge in a brief burst of reminiscence in a hotel foyer, induced by my casual remark that it was a lovely, sunny day outside but that there was a touch of autumn in the air. The illuminating thing was the bewildered look that came into those pale, staring eyes as he talked. It revealed that he was much more touched and troubled by the Why of memory than by the Fact of memory. He was saying, in effect: Why do I remember that? Why do I not remember the other thing? For the first time in his life something within him had gone out of control.

What he started to talk about was a holiday he spent when just under fifteen, in what was at that time called the Queen's County. It had lasted two months, September and October. "Lovely, sunny weather, just like today." What had begun to bother him was not so much that the days had merged and melted together in his memory — after so many years that was only natural — but that here and there, from a few days of no more evident importance than any other days, a few trivial things stuck up above the tides of forgetfulness. And as he mentioned them I could see that he was fumbling, a little fearfully, towards the notion that there might be some meaning in the pattern of those indestructible bits of the jigsaw of his youth, perhaps even some sort of revelation in their obstinacy after so much else had dropped down the crevices of time.

He did not come directly to the major memory that had set his mind working in this way. He mentioned a few lesser memories first, staring out through the revolving glass doors at the sunny street. There was the afternoon when, by idle chance, he leaned over a small stone bridge near his Uncle Bartle's farm and became held for an hour by the mesmerism of the stream flickering through the chickweed. As could happen likewise to a great number of busy men, who normally never think at all about the subjective side of themselves, and are overwhelmed by the mystery of it if once they do advert to it, he attached an almost

magical import to the discovery that he had never forgotten the bright pleasure of that casual hour.

"No, John! Although it must be near sixty years ago. And
I don't believe I ever will forget it. Why is that?"

Of course, he admitted modestly, he had a phenomenal
memory, and to prove it he invited me to ask him the telephone numbers of any half-dozen shops in town. But, yet,
there was that red hay barn where he and his cousin,
Kitty Bergin, played and tumbled a score of times — it was
a blur.

"I can't even remember whether the damn thing was
made of timber or corrugated iron!"

Or there was the sunken river, away back on the level
leas, a stream rather than a river, where one warm September Sunday after Mass he saw, with distasteful pleasure, the men splashing around naked, roughly ducking a
boy who had joined them, laughing at his screams. But,
whereas he also still possessed the soft, surrounding fields,
the imperceptibly moving clouds, the crunch of a jolting
cart far away, the silence so deep that you could have
heard an apple falling, he had lost every detail of the walk
to and from the river, and every hour before and after it. A
less arrogant man might have accepted the simple explanation that the mind wavers in and out of alertness, is bright
at one moment, dim at the next. Those mad, round irises
glared at the suggestion that his mind could at any time
be dim.

He pointed out that he knew the country for miles
around, intimately, walking it and cycling it day after
day: what clung to him of it all, like burs, were mere spots
— a rusty iron gate falling apart, a crossroads tree with a
black patch burnt at its base, an uneventful turn off the
main road, a few undistinguished yards of the three miles of
wall around the local demesne. He laughed scornfully at

my idea that his mind became bright only for those few yards of wall.

"Well, perhaps it became dim then? You were thinking hard about other things up to that point in your walk?"

Here he allowed his real trouble to expose itself. He had not only remembered pointless scraps, but, I found, those scraps had been coming back to him repeatedly during the last few days with a tormenting joy, so that here he was, an old man, fondling nothings as lovingly as if he were fondling a lock of a dead woman's hair. It was plain, at last, that he was thinking of all those fragments of his boyhood as the fish scales of some wonderful fish, never-to-be-seen, sinuous and shining, that had escaped from his net into the ocean.

What had started him off was simple. (I reconstruct it as well as I can, intuiting and enlarging from his own brief, blunt words.) A few mornings before our meeting, fine and sunny also, he had happened to go into a toyshop where they also sold sweets. He was suddenly transfixed by the smell peculiar to these shops — scented soaps, the paint on the tin toys and the sprayed wooden trucks, the smell of the children's gift books, the sweetness of the sweets. At once he was back in that holiday, with his cousin Kitty Bergin, on the leas behind her father's farmhouse (his Uncle Bartle's), one sunny, mistified October morning, driving in a donkey cart down to where his uncle and his cousin Jack were ditching a small meadow that they had retrieved from the rushes and the bog water.

As Kitty and he slowly jolted along the rutted track deeper and deeper into this wide, flat river basin of the Barrow, whose hundreds of streams and dykes feed into what, by a gradual addition, becomes a river some twenty miles away, the two men whom they were approaching looked so minute on the level bog, under the vast sky, that

Dan got a queer feeling of his own smallness in observing theirs. As he looked back, the white, thatched farmhouse nestling into the earth had never seemed so homely, cozy and comforting.

Ferns crackled at the hub. When he clutched one its fronds were warm but wet. It was the season when webs are flung with a wild energy across chasms. He wiped his face several times. He saw dew drops in a row in mid-air, invisibly supported between frond and frond. A lean swathe of mist, or was it low cloud, floated beneath far hills. Presently they saw behind the two men a pond with a fringe of reeds. Against an outcrop of delicately decayed limestone was a bent hawthorn in a cloud of ruby berries. Or could it have been a rowan tree? The sky was a pale green. The little shaven meadow was as lemon-bright as fallen ash leaves before the dew dries on their drifts, so that it would have been hard to say whether the liquid lemon of the meadow was evaporating into the sky or the sky melting down into the field.

They were on a happy mission. Mulvaney the postman had brought two letters to the farmhouse from two other sons: Owen, who was a pit manager in the mines at Castlecomer, and Christopher (who, out of respect, was never referred to as Christy), then studying for the priesthood in a Dublin seminary. Aunt Molly had sent them off with the letters, a jug of hot tea and thick rounds of fresh, homemade bread and homemade apple jam smelling of cloves, a great favorite of Uncle Bartle's. They duly reached the two men, relieved the donkey of bridle, bit and winkers so that he could graze in the meadow, spread sacks to sit on, and while Kitty poured the tea into mugs Bartle reverently wiped his clayey hands on the sides of his trousers and took the letters. As he read them aloud in a slow, singsong voice, like a man intoning his prayers, it was clear that

those two sons had gone so far outside his own experience of the big world that he stood a little in awe of them
both. It was a picture to be remembered for years: the
meadow, the old man, the smoke of the distant farmhouse,
patriarchal, sheltered, simple.

When he laid down the letter from the priest-to-be he
said:

"He's doing well. A steady lad."

When he had read the letter from the mines he said:

"He's doing fine. If he escapes the danger he will go far."

While Jack was reading the letters Kitty whispered to
Danny, thumbing the moon's faint crescent:

"Look! It says D for Danny."

"Or," he murmured to her boldly, "it could be D for
Dear?"

Her warning glare towards her father was an admis-
sion.

"I see here," Jack commented, while his father sucked at
the tea, "that Christopher is after visiting Fanny Emphie.
Her name in religion is Sister Fidelia."

Dan had seen this girl at the Curragh Races during the
first week of his holidays, a neighbor's daughter who, a few
weeks later, entered the convent. He had heard them jok-
ing one night about how she and Christopher had at one
time been "great" with one another. He remembered a
slight, skinny girl with a cocked nose, laughing moist lips
and shining white teeth.

"Read me out that bit," Bartle ordered. "I didn't note
that."

" 'I got special leave from the President to visit Sister
Fidelia, last week, at Saint Joachim's. She is well and
happy but looked pale. She asked after you all. Saint
Joachim's has nice grounds, but the trams pass outside the

wall and she said that for the first couple of weeks she could hardly sleep at all.' "

The two men went on drinking their tea. It occurred to Dan that they did not care much for Fanny Emphie. He saw her now in her black robes walking along a graveled path under the high walls of the convent, outside which the trams at night drew their glow in the air overhead. It also occurred to him, for no reason, that Kitty Bergin might one day think of becoming a nun, and he looked at her with a pang of premonitory loss. Why should any of them leave this quiet place?

"Ha!" said old Bartle suddenly, and winked at Danny, and rubbed his dusty hands and drew out his pipe. This meant that they must all get back to work.

Kitty gathered up the utensils, Danny tackled the donkey, the others went back to their ditching and she and Danny drove back to where the fern was plentiful for bedding. Taking two sickles, they began to rasp through the stalks. After a while she straightened up, so did he, and they regarded one another, waist-deep in the fern.

"Do you think," she asked him pertly, "would I make a nice nun?"

"You!" he said, startled that the same thought had entered their heads at the same time.

She came across to him, slipped from his pocket the big blue handkerchief in which the bread had been wrapped, cast it in an arc about her fair head, drew it tightly under her chin with her left hand, and then with a deft peck of her right finger and thumb cowled it forward over her forehead and her up-looking blue eyes.

"Sister Fidelia, sir," she curtsied, provokingly.

He grappled with her as awkwardly as any country boy, paying the sort of homage he expected was expected

of him, and she, laughing, wrestled strongly with him.
They swayed in one another's arms, aware of each other's
bodies, until she cried, "Here's Daddy," and when he let
her go mocked him from a safe distance for his innocence.
But as they cut the fern again her sidelong glances made
him happy.

They piled the cut fern into the cart, climbed on top of
it, and lay face down on it, feeling the wind so cold that
they instinctively pressed closer together. They jolted out
to the main road, and as they ambled along they talked,
and it seemed to him that it was very serious talk, but he
forgot every word of it. When they came near the crossroads with its little sweetshop, they decided to buy a half-
penny-worth of their favorite sweets, those flat, odd-shaped
sweets — diamonds, hearts, hexagonals — called Conversation Lozenges because each sweet bore on its coarse
surface a ring-posy in colored ink, such as Mizpah, Truth
Tries Troth, Do You Care? or All for Love. Some bore
girls' names, such as Gladys or Alice. His first sweet said,
Yours in Heart. He handed it to her with a smile; she at once
popped it into her mouth, laughing at his folly. As they
ambled along so, slowly, chatting and chewing, the donkey's hooves whispering through the fallen beech leaves,
they heard high above the bare arches of the trees the faint
honking of the wild geese called down from the north by
the October moon.

It was to those two or three hours of that October morning many years ago that he was whirled back as he stood
transfixed by the smells of the sweets-and-toys-shop. For-
getting what he had come there to buy, he asked them if
they sold Conversation Lozenges. They had never heard of
them. As he turned to go he saw a nun leafing through the
children's gift books. He went near her and, pretending to

look at a book, peered under her cowl. To his surprise she was a very old nun. On the pavement he glanced up at the sky and was startled to see there the faint crescent moon. He was startled because he remembered that he had seen it earlier in the morning, and had quite forgotten the fact.

He at once distrusted the message of his memory. Perhaps it was not that the smells had reminded him of little Kitty Bergin eating Yours in Heart, or pretending to be a nun, or wrestling with him in the fern? Perhaps what had called him back was the indifference of those two men to the fate of the nun? Or was there some special meaning for him in those arrowing geese? Or in the cozy, sheltered farmhouse? Maybe the important thing that day had been the old man humbly reading the letters? Why had the two men looked so small under the open sky of the bogland? D, she had said, for Danny . . .

As he stared at me there in the hotel foyer, my heart softened towards him. The pain in his eyes was the pain of a man who has begun to lose one of the great pleasures of life in the discovery that we can never truly remember anything at all, that we are for a great part of our lives at the mercy of uncharted currents of the heart. It would have been futile to try to comfort him by saying that those currents may be charted elsewhere, that even when those revolving glass doors in front of us flashed in the October sun the whole movement of the universe since time began was involved in that coincidence of light. Daniel Cashen of Roscommon would get small comfort out of thinking of himself as a little blob of phosphorescence running along the curl of a wave at night.

And then, by chance, I did say something that comforted him, because as he shook hands with me and said he must be off, I said, without thinking:

"I hope the blankets are doing well?"

"Aha!" he cried triumphantly. "Better than ever."

And tapped his flat-topped hat more firmly on his head and whirled the doors before him out into the sunny street as imperiously as any man accustomed to ordering everything that comes his way.

Through the slowing doors I watched him halt on the pavement. He looked slowly to the right, and then he looked towards his left, and then, slowly, he looked up around the sky until he found what he was looking for. After a few moments he shivered up his shoulders around his neck, looked at the ground at his feet, put his two hands into his pockets, and moved very slowly away, still down-looking, out of sight.

Poor man, I thought when he was gone; rash, blunt, undevious; yet, in his own crude way, more true to life than his famous French contemporary who recaptured lost time only by dilating, inventing, suppressing, merging such of its realities as he could recall, and inventing whatever he could not. Cashen was playing archaeology with his boyhood, trying to deduce a whole self out of a few dusty shards. It was, of course, far too late. My guess was that of the few scraps that he now held in his hands the clue lay not so much in the offer of love and the images of retirement, the girl's courtship, the white farmhouse snuggling down cozily into the earth under the vast dome of the sky, and the old man left behind by his sons, as in the challenging sight of his own littleness on that aqueous plain whose streams barely trickled to the open sea. He said he hadn't thought of it for sixty years. Perhaps not? But he was thinking of it now, when the adventure was pretty well over. As it was. A week later a friend rang me up and said, "Did you hear who's died?" I knew at once, but I asked the question.

He left nearly a hundred and fifty thousand pounds — a lot of money in our country — and, since he never married, he divided it all up among his relatives by birth, most of them comparatively poor people and most of them living in what used to be called, in his boyhood, the Queen's County.

The Younger Generation

When the door closed behind Count Toby the bishop's eyebrows soared. He swiveled back to his desk with a groan, took up his pen, and read the last sentence that he had written an hour ago. Then he shook his head like a dog just come out of a river. The finger with the great amethyst ring began to tap the mahogany. He lifted the edge of his cuff, glanced at his wristlet watch, and said aloud, "Oh, dear, dear!" When he heard the door opening once more he lifted the eyes of a martyr to the ceiling.

"I'm sorry for interrupting you again, my lord," palpitated Count Toby. "I just came back to beg you not to say a word about all this to my wife. And I'm very sorry to have occupied so much of your time. I've talked much too much about my unfortunate affairs. You didn't come to Aughty Castle for *that*. And I'm just sending in Bridie with your egg flip."

He backed out, bumped the jamb, said, "Sorry, sorry," as if he were apologizing to the door. He closed it with a tiny click.

"Ninny!" the bishop grunted, swiveled back, gripped his pen in his fist like a dagger, glared again at what he had written, read it twice, read it three times, exhaled groaningly, and tossed down the pen.

He made yet another effort to concentrate on his pastoral. ". . . and so guide them," he intoned, "to a happy union where their own lives shall repeat this same wonderful cycle of love, marriage and parenthood."

He leaned back and let his eyes wander to the ocean's vast dishes of sunlight. A yacht, miles out, was becalmed in the dead center of one of those circles of sun. His eyes sank to the rocks offshore, pale as pearls. On the second terrace the gardener was softly raking the gravel.

"Such a lovely place!"

He took out his pouch and his pipe and began, pensively, to fill it. The raking stopped. The only sound then was a thrush cracking a snail against a stone, and the bishop chuckling softly and sardonically into his pouch.

"Poor Toby!" he said.

His finger deftly coaxed the shreds into the bowl.

"Still, gentlemen," he murmured into his pouch, "this is going just a little bit too far. I suppose it's fair enough for the laity to treat us as their spiritual doctors. As we are, there's no getting away from it, as we are. But really and truly! And yet, gentlemen, we're told that the first ten years of marriage are the worst? Well, we make many sacrifices, gentlemen, but . . ." He let pouch and pipe sink into his lap and looked out to sea again. "How long can they be . . . It must be twenty years . . ."

Tut-tutting, he resumed the filling of his pipe.

"You know what it is, gentlemen? There's a good deal of truth in the old country saying that the best of wives needs a dose of ashplant medicine now and again. Externally applied, gentlemen. Well laid on, gentlemen. As my old gardener, Philly Cashman, used to say — God be good to him, many a dewy head o' cabbage he stole from me back in County Cavan — 'There's only the wan cure, me lord, for shlow horses and fasht women and that's the shtick!' "

As he lit his pipe he looked through the smoke at his

unfinished pastoral. Hurling away the match, he puffed fiercely, seized the pen, and with concentration wrote a new heading: "Duties of Married People Towards Each Other." He drove on heavily for about five minutes, but it was like pushing a wheelbarrow through mud. There was a knock at the door. The egg flip?

"Come in!"

He achieved another sentence.

"My lord, am I disturbing you?"

He swiveled, and rose.

"Good morning, Miss Burke! I thought it was the maid with my egg flip." He held out his hand. He noticed that she did not kiss the ring. "You weren't down to breakfast? Ah, I see you were out riding."

She might have changed out of her jodhpurs. He admired the handsome, sullen face, the bold wings to the eyebrows; very like the mother; a divil at a point-to-point. She twirled her crop nervously between her fingers.

"My lord, I want to apologize. I mean for last night. It's dreadful that this sort of thing should happen the very first night you stay with us. And you came for rest and —"

She indicated his pastoral with a glance.

"Say nothing at all about it, child. A thing of nothing. These little upsets occur in the best of households. You were just a little upset last night. A bit out of sorts."

The dark head tilted like a frightened race horse. The eyes, dilated, caught the blue of the sky.

"I wasn't apologizing for myself. Mummy has been like that for months past. You must excuse her."

"Your mother is a great credit to your rearing," he said dryly.

She reddened and cried:

"Daddy is a martyr to her; nobody else would stand her for a week."

"My child! My child!"

"But it's perfectly true. I know my own mother. This has been going on for years."

"Miss Anne," he took her trembling hand, "sit down there and listen to me." She took the edge of a chair. "I've known you since you were that high." He smiled at her paternally. "I've known ye all since I was a simple curate in this parish thirty-one years ago. Look now, I'm not going to talk to you like a bishop at all but like an old friend of the family. You're not being quite fair to your mother. She's worried about this marriage of yours."

"Oh, it's natural that you'd take Mummy's side. I quite understand that. It's natural you wouldn't want me to marry a Protestant but . . ."

"Now, that's where you're wrong. It's not at all natural. On the contrary. It's the most natural thing in the wide world for you to fall in love with this young man, why wouldn't you? When a girl is attracted by the twinkle in a young man's eye, or the cock of his head, or whatever else it is that attracts ye in young men" — he invited her smile; she yielded it perfunctorily — "it isn't of his religion she does be thinking. And if a girl does fall in love with a young man, what is more natural than that she should want to marry him? What is more proper, in fact? And, then, Miss Anne, what would be more natural than that I, or any other priest, would want to see that young girl married to the man she loves?"

She stared at him, darting from one eye to the other, in search of the snare.

"But, Miss Anne, we can't live by nature alone."

As he waited for her to appreciate his point, he heard the thrush cracking another snail. In a faint impulse of irritation he remembered the Persian fable about the holy man whose first impulsive desires were all fulfilled, disastrously.

"What I mean is, we sometimes have to resist our natural impulses."

"But," she almost sobbed, "Mummy isn't thinking of anything like that. She wouldn't care if he was a Turk. It's just that she doesn't want me to be married to anybody. She's jealous of me, she always was jealous of me, she hates me, and I hate her, I *do*, I hate her!"

"Oh, dear, dear! You know, Miss Anne . . . The present generation . . . When I was a boy in County Cavan . . . Listen to me! A mother is the best guide any girl could possibly . . . She is wiser in the ways of the world than you are. She's . . ."

She laughed harshly.

"But it isn't true, my lord. Mummy isn't in the least wise. She's got no sense at all. What's the use of pretending? Oh, I do wish, my lord — I'm not being rude or disrespectful — that priests wouldn't always talk to me as if I were a girl of fifteen or a servant in the kitchen. I'm a grown woman. And as for Mummy being better than me, well, the fact of the matter is, you must have seen it for yourself last night, she drinks like a fish. She's tight half the day."

He leaned back and stroked his cheek heavily. He surveyed her coldly.

"Do you love this man very much?"

"Yes."

He detected a shadow of a pause, and peered at her.

"My lord, I hope you won't mind my saying this. It often seems to me that there is . . . that the Church in Ireland . . . that it caters only to the poor and ignorant and there's no place in it for educated people."

"Well, Miss Anne, it may be, it may be. But if there is no

room in the Church for educated people, what is going to happen to poor me?"

She collapsed. He could see her knees trembling. He raised his hand.

"Tell me, my child, do you belong to any club anywhere? Any club? A tennis club? Anything?"

She was on guard again.

"I belong to the Automobile Club in Dublin. It's useful when I go up for a dance and want to change my frock."

"All right. Very well. Now, there are rules in that club, aren't there?"

"Yes. Of course." Watching him carefully.

"And in any other club there are rules? And if you don't like those rules you have to leave the club — or they'll throw you out on your neck. Isn't that so?"

"Ye-e-es. I suppose so."

"And you may go from club to club, but no matter where you halt there are still rules? Aren't there? And," leaning close to her and speaking with all the solemnity in his power, "if you aren't satisfied to obey the rules of any club all you can do is go wandering around the streets like a lost soul. Isn't that so?"

She saw his point. Her eyes fell.

"Isn't that so?" he insisted, almost bullying her.

"In a way . . ."

"Isn't that the whole thing in a nutshell? You want to dodge the rules. Isn't that the holy all of it?"

"I could go to a hotel," she said wildly.

He had to laugh at that.

"Even in a hotel there are rules. I live in a palace. A palace, God help us! Do you think I don't have to toe the line? All you want is your own will and your own way, without regard to the commands of the Church. Be honest, now. Admit it like a brave girl. Isn't that the beginning and end of it?"

"But there are rules and rules, there are sensible rules, in England Catholics are allowed to marry Protestants under dispensation, why should an absolute rule be laid down here?"

"Because I say so," he said severely, and felt his back to the wall. "It is the rule of this diocese. It is *my* rule."

He looked hastily at his desk to indicate that there was no more to be said. He knew what she would try next if he gave her half a chance, and his face darkened as a hundred unpleasant ideas poured into his mind — Gallicanism, *cuius regio*, Modernism, Loisy and Tyrrell and old von Hügel, who barely escaped by the skin of his teeth, the Tutiorists, centuries of dispute, the souls who were lost in heresy, the souls that were barely saved . . .

She made one last effort, her lovely features buttoned up with anger and despair and humiliation.

"But, my lord, if I lived in another diocese this silly rule wouldn't apply to me."

"Silly? Thank you very much, Miss Burke."

"I'm sorry. I'm being rude. I beg your pardon. Our guest. Peace and quietness. The first night . . ."

"No apologies, Miss Anne. We're old friends. Come to me, child, if you are in trouble at any time. I'll pray for you. Now, God help me, I must write my pastoral."

When she shut the door, he sat to his desk, took a new sheet and wrote fast: "Duties of Children to Parents and Superiors." He jotted down guide words. "Obedience. Respect. Discipline. Changing times. Young generation. Church as Wise Guardian. Patience and Understanding." He wrote easily on the last theme.

". . . warm young blood . . . In misunderstanding

their own true motives . . . Yet this spirit of rebellion is sometimes no more than the headstrong impatience of youth, and the Church will gently and kindly guide them from this wayward path back to those sane and wise precepts which the experience of centuries has tested and not found wanting."

He read it aloud, crumpled the page and hurled it into the wastepaper basket.

The yacht was still becalmed in the center of an unruffled circle. The door opened after a faint knock and the maid came in with the egg flip. He relaxed.

"Thanks, Bridie. You *are* Bridie?"

"Yes, Father, I mean my lord." Curtsying.

"Bridie what?"

"Bridie Lynam, my lord." Curtsying.

"That's a familiar name. Where do you come from?"

"West of Cootehill, my lord." Curtsying.

"Ah, no?" In huge, boyish delight. "So you're a Cavan girl? Well, well, isn't that a coincidence! Cootehill? Ah, glory be to God, Cootehill! Well, to be sure and to be sorry." He beamed at her. "Bridie Lynam from Cootehill in the County Cavan. I'm delighted to hear that. Tell me, is it long now since you left Cootehill?"

"Only the two weeks, my lord."

"Only two weeks! Listen" — wallowing back into his chair for a chat. "Is that ould bakery of Haffigan's still at the end of the Main Street?"

"Indeed it is, my lord."

He stared and stared at her, or, rather, at the cerise wall of Haffigan's Steam Bakery, and then he burst out into a peal of laughter, while the girl smiled and squirmed shyly to see the bishop laughing over such a simple thing.

"Well, Bridie Lynam, if I got a pound for every time I

bought a steaming currant loaf at Haffigan's on my way to school! Dear me." He took a sip of his egg flip. "I don't think they put sugar in this, Bridie?"

"Oh, my lord" — red with confusion. "I'll get it, my lord."

"Do, do, and come back and we'll have a little gosther about old times. Haffigan's Steam Bakery!"

Smiling broadly, he went back to his desk, and to his first page, and began to punctuate. Then he began to alter words. He was straightway writing in his best vein on the joy of parents in their first child. A knock.

"Come in, come in," he welcomed and wrote on. He became aware that the countess was speaking to him:

"I'm afraid the egg flip was a bit late, my lord. Anne never told me. She forgets so many things. This room is very close. Let me close the blinds. Were you ever in Venice, my lord?"

"Let them be, please. I like the sun."

As she kept wandering around, patting a pillow, changing the position of a book, tipping a curtain, peering into the garden, he wondered whether her auburn mop was dyed or false.

"Yes! The sun. The sunflower to the sun." She looked around her distractedly. "Anne adores the sun. She lies in it all day long. Strange girl. I do hope everything is all right? I simply cannot get trained servants nowadays. I often long for the old days when one whipped one's serfs."

Suddenly she swooped on her knees before him, and burst into a loud sobbing wail:

"Oh, my lord, help me! Everybody in this house hates me. Everybody is plotting against me. My daughter hates me. I haven't a friend in the world. What will I do? What will I do?" The bishop looked wildly around him. Her wail became piercing. She clawed at his coattails. "They all think I'm just a stupid, blowzy old woman! Day and night, my lord, they are at me!"

Count Toby opened the door and with a look of shame and agony he said, very gently, "Mary, dear?" The bishop helped her to her feet. With sudden, monstrous dignity she walked out. The count looked miserably at the bishop and closed the door.

The bishop stared at the door until Bridie Lynam came in with the sugar bowl, pale and flustered.

"Thank you, Bridie," he whispered. As she was about to go, he decided to add: "I hope you'll be happy here. Nice place. The count is a grand man. One of the old stock."

"Yes, my lord." She added: "I'm leaving next week, my lord. I'm goin' to England."

He turned his back on her. The yacht was still there.

"That's a long way away. Have you friends there?"

"Yes, my lord" — softly.

He kept his back to her so that she might not feel shy and asked:

"Is there a boy there?"

Her "Yes, my lord" was so soft he hardly heard it.

"Irish boy?"

"From Cootehill, my lord."

He sighed.

"They're all going," he murmured to himself.

He remained for so long looking out at the scallop of clouds along the horizon that when he turned the room was empty. He sat to his desk again. He moved his papers aside. Drawing another clean sheet towards him, he leaned his head on his hand and began to write a letter.

"My Dearest Darling Mother, I often think how kind the good God has been to me to have given me so good a mother. Since I first knelt at your lap to say my prayers

. . ." He wrote on quietly. "And as it was you who welcomed me home from school so it was to you that I returned every year from college . . ." He wrote on, finished the page and signed it, "Your loving son, Danny." Then he took the sheet and very carefully, very deliberately, tore it into tiny fragments and let them flutter like snow into the basket.

Then he cupped his face in his hands and whispered, like a prayer, "Tomorrow I'll say Mass for the respose of your dear soul." Wearily he resumed his pastoral letter, and now it wrote itself quietly and simply. But as he wrote he felt no joy or pride in it, no more than if this, too, were a letter not to the living but to the dying and the dead. He was not interrupted again. By lunchtime he had finished the first draft. Only Count Toby came to lunch. They talked of old friends and old times. After a while the bishop said, gently, "Perhaps, Toby, do you think it might be better, conceivably, if I were to leave this afternoon?"

Toby glanced up at him under his sad Spaniel's eyebrows.

"Perhaps so, Danny."

The bishop nodded and began to talk, at random, about the cemetery of Père Lachaise and the wildfire that runs at night along the cemetery paths. The count stirred his coffee in silence: he was remembering how he had taken Anne there when she was fifteen, and how lovely she had looked as she threw herself into his arms at the sight of a little leaping tongue of blue fire among the immortelles on a grave.

"Anne," he said after a long time, "has just told me that she is going to take a flat in Dublin."

"Ha!" said the bishop. "So she's trying a new club?"

"How is that?" asked Count Toby.

"Ah, nothing! Nothing."

Love's Young Dream

I don't remember my first visits to that part of Ireland, although my father often told me that since I was four years old I used to be sent there every year, sometimes twice a year. He was a ship's captain, my mother had died when I was three, and whenever he was at sea and no nearer relative could have me I would be sent off for safe-keeping to the County Kildare.

The first visit I remember at all clearly was when I was ten, to my Uncle Gerry's farm near the town of Newbridge. I remember it because it was during this visit that Noreen Coogan pushed me into the Liffey. (Noreen was the only child of my aunt's servant, Nancy Coogan; that year she must have been about twelve or thirteen.) I can still see myself standing dripping on the bank, crying miserably, and my uncle assuring me that Noreen —"The bold, bad slut!"— would be kept far away from me for the rest of the holidays; at which I began to wail more loudly than before, and he, guessing the state of my heart, began to laugh so loudly at me that I fairly bawled.

I have no clear image of what Noreen looked like at the time, or, indeed, at any later time. All I have clearly in my memory is a vision of a cloud of corn-fair hair, and two large cornflower eyes, and for some reason or other, I always want to say that she had a complexion like sweet peas. Perhaps I saw her at some time with a big bunch of cream-and-pink sweet peas in her arms, or standing in a garden with a lot of sweet peas in it, and felt that the delicate blend of colors and scents was a perfect setting for her. But all my memories of those early visits are like that — both actual and dim, like the haze of heat that used to soften the fair surface of the far meadows across the river, or the swarms of gnats rising and sinking hazily over the reeds below the bridge. I am sure I saw my uncle's stable-man, Marky Fenelon, quite clearly, a little man with a face all composed of marbles, from his blackberry eyes to his crumpled chin or his tightly wound ears; but when I heard that he was a Palatine I never asked what it meant and did not care. I was very clearly aware of Nancy Coogan, big, bustling, bosomy, bare-armed and with a laugh like a thunderclap, but when I gathered somehow that she and Marky were courting and would marry some day all that this *some day* meant to me was Never. Is all childhood made up of facts of nature that are accepted beyond questioning? Perhaps mine was prolonged. When I was thirteen I was so vague as to what marrying meant that I much amused Nancy by asking her why some ladies are called Miss and some Mrs. She laughed and said the misses are the ones that miss, which I thought very clever indeed.

One reason why Noreen and my clearer memories of Newbridge go together is that she focused my holidays for me. She was their one clear center from which everything went outward and to which everything returned. For after I was ten she became as certain and fixed a part of those visits as my first sight of the elongated Main Street of Newbridge, with the walls of the cavalry barracks all along one side of it and the sutlers' shops all along the other; or the peaceful sound of the gun wagons jingling along the dusty roads — they suddenly sounded less peaceful the year the Great War broke out; or the happy moment of ar-

rival at the farm when I would run to meet Marky Fenelon
in the wide, cobbled yard and at once hand him his
ritual present of a pound of sailor's twist, bought for him
by my father; or — one of the happiest moments of all —
when I would run into the flagged kitchen to Nancy with
her ritual present, which was always a lacy blouse bought
in some port like Gibraltar, or Naples or Genoa. At the
sight of me she would let out a welcoming roar of laughter,
squash me up against her great, soft, bulging bosom, give
me a smacking kiss and lift me, laughing and shrieking,
high in the air until my head nearly touched the ceiling.

It was the year in which I asked my famous question
about the difference between misses and missuses that I
also felt the first faintest, least stir of questioning interest in
Nancy's and Marky's marathon courtship. It was really no
more than an idle question and I had only a small interest
in the answer. That day she was making soda bread on the
kitchen table and I was sitting up on the end of the table
watching her knead and pound the dough.

"Nancy!" I said pertly. "What's up with you at all that
you're not marrying Marky? When are you going to marry
him? Marry him tomorrow, Nancy! Go on, Nancy! Will you
marry him tomorrow?"

She let out one of her wild laughs and began to scrape
the dough from her fingers and fling the scrapings down on
the kneading board, saying gaily with each flap of her
hands:

"This year! Next year! Sometime! Never!"

"Is it the way, Nancy, that you're not in love with
Marky?"

This time her laughter was a quarry blast.

"God love you, you poor child, that has nothing at all
to do with it. It's just that he doesn't like having Noreen
living with us. Now, go off and play with the cat," she

added crossly, and began to carve a deep cross into the flattened loaf. At once I wanted to stab her cake myself and began begging her for the knife. Anyway, this talk about Noreen and Marky merely meant what I had always known, that they would all be always there waiting for me at the start of every holiday.

One reason why I know I was thirteen that year was that the next time I went to stay with Uncle Gerry I was fifteen, and this I know because I very soon found out that those two extra years made a great difference to all of us. What made the difference was that in my fourteenth year I spent a long summer spell with my three Feehan cousins, some seven or eight miles away from the Newbridge farm over on the plain of the Curragh. There I had another uncle, Ken Feehan, who had some sort of job in connection with the racecourse.

The Curragh is famous for two things, its racecourse on one side of the plain and on the other the extended military settlement, which seems to outline the farthest edge of green with the long faint stroke of a red pencil. This settlement is still known as the Camp, long after its original tent canvas has been transformed into barrack squares in red brick, wooden huts, tin chapels and tin shops. Sheltering belts of stunted firs have now been planted along its entire length to protect it from the bitter winds blowing down from the mountains, whose slow drum roll closes the view to the southeast. From the door of my Uncle Ken's house, a long, whitewashed cottage or bungalow near the grandstand, we looked southeast at the far-off red pencil-line across a rolling expanse of short grass, empty except for a few cropping sheep, scattered tufts of furze and an occasional car slowly beetling along the road that crosses the Curragh from Newbridge to the south.

It was an empty place for three girls to live in. It is also

to the point that the plain is of great age. The couple of
roads that cross it are the old woolpack roads into Danish
Dublin. It is known that the distant finger of the round
tower of Kildare, to the west, was gray with age in the
twelfth century. There was a racecourse here some two
thousand years ago. Weapons of the Stone Age have been
dug up in various parts of the plain. I like to think of this
silent antiquity whenever I think of Philly, the eldest of
my three cousins, standing at night at the door of the
cottage — it is the way I always remember her now — staring across the plain at the only thing there that really interested her, the remote lights of the military camp.
Whether the Camp had always excited her or not I do not
know, but when I first met her, after the outbreak of the
war, everything about it did — the news of departing
or arriving regiments, the crackle of gunfire from the pits,
the distant flash of a heliograph on bright days, the faint
sound of regimental bands borne to us on the south-
easterly wind. Standing there at the cottage door, she
would talk endlessly of all the handsome and brave poor
boys fighting and falling at that very moment on the plains
of Flanders. She inferred the whole war from the flash of a
mirror, the short rattle of rifle fire, the faint beating of
drums, a wavering bugle call. She was eighteen.

I have no doubts at all about Philly's looks. She was not
pretty but she was not plain. I grant that her nose was a
bit peaky, her teeth slightly prominent, her figure almost
skinny; but she had two lively brown eyes like an Italian
girl, and her dark, shining hair was combed slick back
from her prominent profile with the effect of a figurehead
on a ship's prow. Her lower lip was always moistened by
her upper teeth, her hands were nervous, her laughter
on a hair trigger, her moods unpredictable and turning as
rapidly as a trout in a stream; and she was a magnificent

liar. This, I see, is as much an implication of her nature as a description of her appearance, but it is how she struck everybody who met her — an unflattering impression dispelled completely in one second.

That I have no wish to do more than mention her two sisters, Moll and Una, may suggest further the force of her personality. She overshadowed them completely, although both of them were capable and pleasing girls. She bullied Moll all the time and she forced all the housework on her simply by refusing to do her own share of it. Poor Moll, a soft, rotund, pouting girl, was no match for her and never did anything in self-defense except complain feebly, weep a little, then laugh despairingly and with a wag of her bottom go on cheerfully with her double chores. Philly did not need to bully Una, a gentle, fair-flaxen girl of about my own age — she was too young and delicate for bullying, cycled into Newbridge every day to school at the local convent, and studied endlessly when at home. I think she had realized very early that the cottage was a place to get out of as quickly as possible.

I liked the three of them, but I far preferred Philly. She was more fun, and I liked the streak of boyish devilment in her that always made her ready for any escapade. I suppose she suffered me as being better company than none, and I also suppose that the main thing in my favor was that although a child to her eyes I was at least male. This is not merely an unkind remark. Her reputation had preceded my meeting with her. Back in Newbridge the general attitude to her was that she was a foolish virgin. At the mention of her name my Uncle Gerry had just phewed out a long, contemptuously good-humored breath. My aunt laughed at her. Once she made the witty and shrewd remark: "That girl has far too many beaus to her string." Nancy sniffed mockingly, "That featherhead!"; but she may have jealously compared her to her own adored Noreen. Marky said, "Aha! A bold lassie!" Noreen was, by turns, respectfully and scornfully silent, but, young as I was, I smelled envy.

As for her own sisters, they admired her and feared her and did not love her. They assured me privately that her list of boys was as long as my arm. ("Boys" was a popular word at that time — the "boys" at the Front, our "boys" in Flanders, and so on.) Their list included a rich trainer from the County Meath, a subaltern from the Camp, a jockey, a farmer from behind Kildare, a publican's son in Newbridge, a young lawyer from Dublin, even a stable-boy from the stables of one of the wealthy trainers who, then as now, lived in half-timbered houses all around the edge of the plain behind white rails and clipped privet hedges. I gathered that all of these beaus were met on race days, in the enclosure, on the members' stand, in the restaurant, to all of which places, because of her father, she had complete access. There was more than a suggestion that she met her admirers on varying terms, playing whatever role pleased her fancy and suited their class. Certainly, those days when everybody of her own class swarmed on the open plain outside the rails and only the comparatively few paid to go inside them, the daughter of an employee of the Turf Club would have had to present herself very well indeed to be accepted by a lieutenant, a lawyer or a trainer.

I was torn this way and that by her. In loyalty to Newbridge I knew I should think her a figure of fun, and I could see that she was a little bully and a shrew, but she would sweep me off my feet whenever she started to talk about that Camp, whose lights flickered at night across an empty plain. She turned it into a magic doorway to the world. In Newbridge, everything, I have said, had been actual but hazy. When she talked to me about the real world I heard Life begin to paw its stable floor.

"Listen, lad! When you grow up take the King's shilling! Be a soldier! See the world!" And then, with her wide, wild, white-toothed laugh: "Or, if it has to be, see the next world!"

I shall never have a dim or hazy notion of Philly Feehan as long as I remember the baking day when the four of us stood at the door of the cottage, the racecourse behind us as empty as a ballroom on the morning after a dance, the plain before us as empty as a bed at noon, and watched a small, slow cloud of dust move at marching pace from the Camp towards the railway station at Kildare, and heard the clear rattle of the parting snare drums. She shocked us all by suddenly crying out with passion, her brown eyes fixed on the little creeping dust cloud, her face pale under her shiny, black coif:

"I wish to God Almighty I was a bloody hussar!"

She taught me how to smoke. I drank my first beer with her in a hotel bar across the plain in Kilcullen. She gave me my first lesson in dancing. Looking back at her now, I see why her type of girl was the ideal of the soldiers of the Nineteen-fourteen War. They had been made to think of themselves as "boys." Their ideal woman was the young virgin, still with her hair down, the Flapper, a blend of devilment and innocence — their most highly desired antithesis to rain-filled trenches, mud above their puttees, and shells whining and exploding over their heads all day long.

So, you can guess why my next visit to Newbridge was different from any that went before. I was now turned fifteen. Noreen was eighteen. The others were beyond the years. They behaved to me as always, but I was not the same with them. I had become wary. It began the minute I arrived. When my Uncle Gerry drove the old tub-trap into the cobbled yard through the big tarred gates opened by Marky immediately he heard the familiar clop of the pony coming along the road, I handed the ritual pound of twist over the side to Marky, alighted, asked the usual questions, said "I suppose ye're not married yet?" and then, as if on an afterthought, "Oh, and how's our little Noreen these days?"

She must have done something to annoy him specially that day because he said grimly and shortly:

"Oh, very well, I believe! A bit rakish, now and again! But very well. In the best of health."

I was alert at once.

"In what way rakish, Marky?" I laughed innocently.

"Ah!" He shook his head upward. If he had been a horse I would have heard the rattle of the bit and seen the yellow teeth. "I suppose it might be through having no father to keep her in order."

I nodded in sage agreement.

"How long is it now, Marky, since he died?"

He was untackling the pony, detaching the traces from the hames, his face against the pony's neck, but though I could not see him I knew from his voice that he was not going to pursue the subject.

"Well!" he growled into the pony's back. "It was all a long time ago. Nancy's inside expecting you."

He could hardly have said it plainer. I went indoors to her and produced the usual Italian blouse. She hugged me and kissed me, but I was too grown-up now to be lifted to the ceiling, and I hugged her back hard and thought she had fine eyes and was a damn handsome woman yet. Finally I said it:

"And how's Noreen these days?"

She turned back to the table and gently lifted the white silk blouse and said in a thick, cozy voice:

" 'Tis lovely. 'Twill suit Noreen down to the ground."

"But," I protested, "it's for you! My father sent it for you."

"Tshah! What do I want with finery? I'm gone beyond fineries. But," smiling fondly, and lifting up the blouse again by the points of the shoulders to look it all over, "Noreen will look a masher in that."

No age is at once so insensitive and so sensitive as adolescence. It is one reason why young people are so exasperating to adults. I looked at her with curiosity, oblivious of her maternal devotion, and elegantly leaning against the table I ventured:

"Nancy! If you were married the three of ye would be as happy as three kittens in a basket. And Marky would be a father to Noreen."

She dropped the blouse in a silken heap, gave me a sharp look and flounced to the fireplace.

"Noreen," she said to the range, banging in the damper, "doesn't want him as long as she has me! Anyway, since he won't have both of us he can have neither of us. Have you seen your aunt yet? She'll be expecting you."

The flick of her skirt frightened me. I did not know what I had touched, but it felt red-hot. All I knew was that this prolonged courtship of theirs was going, if not gone, on the rocks.

That first day I did not run down the road in search of Noreen as I would have done two years before. I walked down to where Coshea's Boreen comes out on River Road and I came on her there, beyond the laundry, leaning over the wall, showing the hollow backs of her knees, chewing a bit of straw, looking across the river at the meadows and the Dublin road beyond them. I stole up behind her,

slipped my arm about her waist and said gaily, "Hello,
Sis!"

She just glanced at me and said:

"Do you mind removing your arm?"

"Oho!" Very loftily. "Touch me not, eh?"

I was so mad I could have spat in her eye, but I pre-
tended nothing — I would not give her that much satisfaction. Instead, I started chatting away about what I
had been doing since I saw her two summers ago. She kept
chewing the straw and looking idly across the river. I do
not remember what precisely I said that made her begin
to pay heed to me except that it was my idea of a gentle
probe about Marky and her mother, but it made her give
me a slow, mocking smile that said, as plainly and scornfully as if she had spoken the actual words of an American
phrase that was beginning to be current at the time: "Well,
and what do you know?" — meaning that I had surprised
her, and that I knew nothing, not only about Marky and
her mammy but about Everything in General, and that I
could bloody-well stop pumping her and go away and
find it all out for myself the way she had done. I expected
her to say at any moment, "Hump off, kid!" She conveyed
it silently. Women do not talk to small boys.

If I had had any pride I would have walked away from
her. But at fifteen years and a couple of months you are so
frantic to know all about Everything in General that you
have no pride, only lots of cunning. I said, very sadly:

"I suppose, Noreen, you think I'm only a kid?"

"How old are you?" she asked, with just a faint touch of
sympathy in her voice.

"Going on to sixteen. But everybody," I said bitterly,
"talks to me as if I were still ten. Have a fag?"

I flashed out my new mock-silver cigarette case. I observed with satisfaction the way she glanced down the

road towards the bridge and the end of the Main Street, and then turned and leaned her back on the wall and glanced idly up Cat Lane before saying, in a bored voice:

"I suppose, really, I might as well."

I noted also that she smoked the way all girls smoke who are not smokers, continually corking and uncorking her mouth. I kept up the role of downtrodden youth:

" 'Tis well for you, Noreen. I only wish I was eighteen. You can do what you like. My da would leather hell out of me if he caught me smoking. The way he talks to me about my stamina and my muscles you'd think he wants me to be another Jack Johnson. Would Nancy be cross with you?"

"I'd like to see her!" she boasted.

"I know a girl in Dublin who smokes thirty a day."

This was too much for her.

"You know nothing about girls!"

"Oho! We grow up fast in Dublin!"

I blew smoke down my nose and turned around and leaned over the river wall and spat in the river. She also turned and blew smoke down her nose and spat in the river. For a moment or two she looked across at the golden meadows. Then:

"I'm engaged to be married."

I was shocked upright.

"You can't be! Not at eighteen! You're too young!"

"I won't get married for a year or two, of course. But I'll get married when I'm twenty. You don't think I'm going to hang around here tied to my ma's apron strings all my bloomin' life?"

"Where's your engagement ring?"

"It's a secret yet," she said, with another slow, hot look.

I looked at her for a while, torn between disbelief and a disappointment that had something in it of despair. Then I

let my cigarette fall into the river. It was like a fellow
throwing down his gun. She said:

"Come on and we'll walk down by the weirs."

I walked by her side until we came to a hawthorn in full
spate, listening to her telling me all about her boy. He was
a sergeant on the Curragh. He cycled over from the Camp
whenever he was off duty and she went out to meet him
halfway. He was not going to remain a sergeant for long;
he was "going for an officer," and when he got his commission they would live in London. I asked her if Nancy
knew about all this. It was the only thing I said that upset
her.

"If you say one word to her," she threatened, "I'll cut the
thripes out of you."

After a bit I risked saying:

"If he saw us together now would he be jealous?"

She was pleased to laugh, condescendingly.

"I'd love to see him jealous. He's simply mad about me."

And she drowned me with talk of the life she was having
now as his "belle," and the life she would have after she
was married, until it was I who became mad with jealousy.
Do you doubt it? Even if I *was* only fifteen and three
months? Dear Heaven! Does nobody in the world know
how old it is to be fifteen and three months? Whenever
now I see a group of boys returning, say after holidays, to
school, of any age between twelve and eighteen, I look
most carefully into their faces in search of eyes that cor-
respond to my unalterable concept of fifteen and three
months. I look at myself through those eyes. I see my own
frustration in them. For how can anybody who has to come
close to them not feel their helplessness? Each of them is
imprisoned in childhood and no one can tell him how to
escape. Each of them must, blind-eyed, gnaw his way out,
secretly and unaided. That they may be the eyes of boys

who are mathematically fourteen, seventeen, even (I have met them) nineteen does not matter. All that matters is the fear of being on a brink and not knowing what is beyond it. At certain moments all through our lives we touch a point where ignorance is teetering on the brink of some essential revelation which we fear as much as we need it. These brinks, these barriers, these *No Road* signs recur and recur. They produce our most exhausting and hateful dreams. They tell us every time that we have to be born all over again, grow, change, free ourselves yet once again. Each teetering moment is as terrible as the imaginary point of time in Eastern philosophy when a dying man, who knows that within a few seconds he will be reincarnated, clings to life in terror of his next shape or dies in the desire to know it. The particular tenderness attaching to the age which I call fifteen-and-three-months is that it is the first of many such steps and trials and must affect the nature of all that follow.

Since that July I have been in love half a dozen times, but I have never felt anything since like the tearing torment of those few weeks of summer. How I used to fawn on this creature, whose beauty, I now know, was an illusion! How I used to flatter this girl, whom, I was so soon to realize, I should never have trusted, merely to be allowed to sit beside her and secretly feel the edge of her skirt!

"And does he take you to many dances in the Camp, Noreen? But where do you get the dance dresses? I'd love to see you dressed for a dance! You must look smashing! But where do you get this little card that you write the dances on? Did you say that it is a pink pencil that's attached to it? By a pink thread? You didn't *really* mean, did you, Noreen, that they have *six* wineglasses?"

Her least word could crush me like a moth. But from that summer on she had a power over all of us that was

like a tyrant's. One night when Nancy flounced in with
the supper and banged down the teapot, and whisked out
again with a flick of her tail, my uncle said crossly, "What's
up with that one now?" — implying that things had been
"up with" her before now; my aunt shot a glance at me and
said, "Our ladyship is gone to the pictures without taking
Nancy. And Marky is gone off to a whist drive." I wonder
they didn't notice me. Cinema, indeed! I saw the road to
the Curragh, dark, secret, scented. Thinking of that sergeant, I must have had eyes like two revolvers. Yet I never
realized the extent of Nancy's miseries and suspicions until,
one day, she frightened me by saying:

"What are you always mooning about for by yourself?
You have no life in you at all this year. Was it you I saw
wandering out the road by yourself the other night?"

I knew then that she also had been wandering along the
roads at dark, searching for her lamb.

For three whole despairing weeks I did not see Noreen
at all. Then, quite suddenly, one Sunday morning I collapsed at Mass. My uncle's doctor diagnosed my illness as
acute anemia, but I am satisfied now that it was a trau-
matic illness. On August the ninth I was sent home. My
father got three months' leave to be near me, and I remained
at home under his care for the rest of the summer and most
of the autumn. Then, towards the end of October, I began
to get a bit brighter in myself when he said that I should
go to the Feehans and he would join me there for Christmas with his brother Kenneth, whom he had not seen for
some years. I argued to myself that Newbridge would be
only a few miles away and that I could more tactfully spy
out the land from the slopes of the Curragh. As it happened, things turned out very differently from the way
I expected.

I had not reckoned with the weather. To understand this, you should see the place as I did that November. In the winter the Curragh seems older and wider. The foggy air extends its size by concealing its boundaries. The grass is amber, as if from the great age of the plain. For one week that November a sprinkle of snow fell almost every day, so that all the bottoms were white and the crowns of their slopes were melted green. At dusk the whole plain seemed to surge against the glimmering cliffs of the distant Camp and only the lights of a traveling car would then restore the earth to its natural solidity. In the cottage life became as restricted as aboard a ship. Only easygoing Moll was content, her tubby figure always moving busily through the pale glow of the house.

On most days there was little to do but watch the horses at the morning workouts — whenever a horse halted steam enveloped its jockey — or, if the air cleared, walk across to the Camp. It was always Philly who proposed this expedition — no other walk appealed to her — even if we did nothing when we got there except buy some trifle at the stores, such as the latest copy of the *Strand* or the *Red Magazine,* or, if she had the money, she might treat herself to a small bottle of scent. Her favorite, I remember, was some allegedly Oriental perfume called Phul-Nana. We might go into the red-painted tin chapel to say a prayer for the boys. Its candles were as calm as light that had gone to sleep, its tin roof creaking faintly in the wind.

I had always thought the Camp a bleak and empty place. During the winter it was as blank and cold as a plate of sheet iron, and as silent as an abandoned factory building. One wondered where all the soldiers were. It was so silent that it was startling to hear a lorry zooming up the hill towards the tower with its Union Jack hanging soggily from the flagstaff. After the lorry had passed into the Camp there was a ghostliness about the long tracks that it had left behind it on the slight snow. Noreen had talked about "all the fun" that took place here in the winter. When I asked Philly where all the fun was, she said crossly that it all took place at night. I could only imagine, or over-imagine, its supposed liveliness at those hours when she and I would stand in the porch of the cottage gazing fixedly at its flickering until the cold defeated her curiosity and desire.

After about three weeks I suddenly began to feel one night that something had happened between us, standing there under the porch, watching those distant fireflies, sometimes talking, sometimes hardly speaking at all. At first it had the feeling of some form of complicity or collusion. I even wondered whether it might not be that the years between us had dwindled since I last stayed in the cottage. She had been eighteen then. I had been fourteen, divided from her by childhood. Now that she was twenty and I on the brink of sixteen there was barely a rivulet between us. I noted too that she had recently begun to converse more seriously with me. Perhaps that was merely because she was bored, or perhaps it was because I no longer felt obliged by loyalty to Newbridge to think of her as a comic figure, and so felt a greater sympathy with her. She continued to impress me in other ways. The season induced her to do something else that she had never done during the summer: to practice on the old upright Collard and Collard, with its pale-green, fluted satin shining behind its mahogany fretwork. Its strings sounded very tinkly during that snowy week. During the thaw they jangled. One night I found her reading, pencil in hand, and asked, "What's the book?" It was Moran's *French Grammar*. She was trying unaided to learn the language. I noted the books she was reading — histories, travel books, famous biographies. She borrowed most of these from a widow, much older than herself, living in Kildare, a colonel's widow, whom she had met by chance at one of the meetings on the Curragh.

After I had heard about the colonel's widow I guessed the truth. With the diabolical shrewdness of my age I saw that she was playing, for me, the part of a woman of a certain age with nothing left for her to do but to encourage a young man who still had the world before him. She once said, "Ah! If I only had my life to live over again!" But, in the end, this pretending to be so much older than she was worked directly opposite to her intentions. In her sense of the dramatic difference between our ages she let down all her defenses, as if she were a very, very old lady thinking, "Nothing that I can say can possibly matter from one so old to one so tender." The result was inevitable. When a passionate sigh or a deliberate profanity led her to expose her hand I, quietly, read her hand and excited by what I saw encouraged her without guile. In proportion as she responded to the rising sap of my wonder she lapsed into sincerity and I achieved equality. It was for this unguarded moment that I was lying in wait, as my earlier experience with Noreen had taught me that I must if I wished to be treated as an equal.

I think she first realized how far she had lowered her defenses the night when, as we sat alone over the parlor fire — Moll was singing in the kitchen, Uncle Ken in bed with his rheumatics and Una studying in her bedroom — I looked at her after she had told some wildly romantic story of army life in India and said, in a tone of voice with which I hoped her older admirers had made her familiar:

"Philly, you have lovely hair. I'm sorry you put it up since I was here before. I'd love to see you letting it all ripple down your back."

I knew by the start she gave and the abrupt way she said, "My hair is all right," that she had recognized the tone. When I kept looking at her with a curved smile and lowering eyes, I was gratified to see the frightened look in her eyes. It meant that I was able to interest her not as a boy but as a man, so that I was merely amused to see her trying to flounder back quickly to the role of the grown woman talking graciously to the young boy.

I was content with this new situation for about a week: that is to say, I played the role of the sixteen-year-old pupil with a twenty-year-old teacher who knows that he is attracted by her, but who feels that it is as much her duty to keep him in his place as it is her pleasure to hold his admiration. Suddenly, I got tired of it. One night, in a temper at some correction she had made, I shut the book with a bang, glared at her, and said that I preferred to work alone.

"But," she smiled sweetly, "I only want to *help* you!"

"I don't want you to *help* me!" I cried haughtily.

"Believe me, my child," she said sarcastically, "you need a great deal of help."

"Not from you!" I retorted.

"Master Know-all!"

"And I'm not a child!"

"You are a schoolboy."

I screamed at her:

"I'm not. I'm not. I'm not."

She flew into a rage herself.

"Be quiet! Remember that if you can't behave yourself you can't stay here!"

I swept the books from the table, and raced out of the parlor, and the cottage, into the garden, and so through the wicket gate straight on to the darkness and emptiness of the plain.

The night was frosty. Not only the Camp but the whole hollow plain was an iron dish. But I was not aware of the cold as I walked straight ahead, as hot with anger as a man might be with alcohol — that anger of resentment which makes young people cry at the very injustice of being born. It began to die in me only as the exhaustion induced by constant stumbling in the dark, the splendor of the sky, the magnitude of the plain and the cold night air worked on me to cool my rage and fan my desire.

I lay down under the shelter of a furze clump, between the Camp lights and the cottage lights. Once I thought I heard the coughing of a sheep. Then I realized that I was hearing only the wind rattling through some withered thistles near my feet. The wind, the darkness, the stars, the lights, the size of the plain dwindled me and isolated me. My isolation turned all these human and sky-borne lights into my guides and companions. When my head rolled to the north to the lone cottage, to the south to the wind-washed campfires, and looked straight up to the stars of the Charioteer, I remember shouting out in my excitement, without knowing what I meant, "The lights! The lights!" — as if I wanted some pyrotechnic convulsion in nature to occur, some flashing voice to speak. Only the wind whispered. Only the dried thistles coughed.

It was long after midnight when I re-entered the garden. The cottage was quiet. She would have heard the sweetbrier squeaking over the porch, the soft snoring of her daddy, and after a little while, her bedroom door being opened. She must have thought it was Moll, because she said nothing. I heard her gasp when my hand fell on her bare arm, and I whispered:

"It's me, Philly."

She sat up, whispering, "What's wrong?" and I heard her fumbling with the matches.

"Don't light a light!" I begged.

"What is wrong?" she whispered again, and the rest of our talk was carried on in whispering in the dark.

"Philly, I don't want to fight with you."

"That's all right, we both lost our tempers."

"I'm very fond of you, Philly."

"So am I, of you. Good night, now."

"But I'm not a schoolboy."

"Yes, yes. Go to your room now. Daddy will be raging if he hears you."

"Philly! You are a grown woman. And I am *not* a boy."

"I only said it to tease you."

"Philly!" I could feel my heart pounding.

"Yes?"

"Kiss me!"

"If you don't go back to bed at once I will call Molly."

"If you don't kiss me I'll run out of the house and never come back again. Never! Never again!"

(She said that my voice rose: "You were sort of gasping. You were threatening me. I was sure daddy would hear.")

"If I give you one kiss will you go right back to bed?"

I still feel that first kiss, her parted lips, the gateways of the world opening, the stars over the plain shivering, the wind blowing, and her terror as she said:

"Now go!"

"Another!"

She struck a match, lit her candle, and saw me in my pants, shirt and bare feet. She started to upbraid me, but I saw that she saw at a glance that she was no longer dealing with a boy. I sat on the side of her bed, filled with wonder and delight at her bare shoulders and her dark, shining hair down about them, and the knowledge that she was not looking at me as a boy nor speaking to me as a boy. She gripped my hand and she assured me that in future I

would have to keep to myself or leave the house, that she
knew now that she had been stupid and foolish to have
treated me as a boy, because any woman should have
known better, but that she understood now and she hoped
I understood, so would I please realize that I was a man
and behave like a man? And as she whispered, like this, so
seriously, I stroked her bare forearm, and felt the trembling of it and the weakness entering into it, and so must
she because she stretched out her clenched knuckles to
the wall.

"I am going to call Molly!"

"Just one last kiss?" I begged, staring at the whiteness of
her neck and bosom.

Still holding her knuckles to the wall:

"On your word of honor, you will go then?"

"On my word of honor."

When we parted, two hours later, she upbraided me
with a gentleness that affected me far more than anything
else that had happened since our quarrel in the parlor.

I lay awake until I heard the cock crowing. I felt no
triumph. My delight was chastened by its own wonder. If
she thought that I was in love with her she was deluded.
I was too supremely astonished by my adventure to be fully
aware of her, and when we met in the morning and I
looked at her as if she were a mirror I did not recognize
myself. Totally unaware that what appealed to her in me
was my utter innocence, taking her to be a woman who
had seen strange places, known strange people, heard
strange things that I had never seen, known or heard,
fearing that she was aware only of my utter inexperience,
I behaved unnaturally and self-consciously, hurting her
cruelly by what I considered were the proper airs of any
man of the world on such occasions. I spoke coolly to her,

smiled cynically, once I even winked at her. Whatever I did I knew that I must conceal my ignorance from her; for during those two hours, lying close together, we had been as harmless as doves, as innocent as lambs, simply because I — as I thought then, but as I see now both of us — had not known what else to do.

Besides, I now needed above everything else a retirement into silence, secrecy, self-contemplation, spiritual digestion, a summoning of shocked resources. I put on my cap after breakfast, borrowed one of my uncle's walking sticks, put a cigarette into the side of my mouth, waved a "Tol-lol" to the three girls, and spent the whole day wandering, blind and lost, about the back roads that lead into the great central bogland of Ireland, an earth-lake of purple heather, where you might tramp all day and see nothing stir except a snipe rising with a whir or, far away, a sloping pillar of blue peat-smoke from a turf-cutter's fire. Its emptiness suited my sense of lostness. I had no wish to arrive anywhere. I wanted to remain undestined. All I wanted was that my other lost self should come back to me. In much the same spirit I so obviously avoided every chance of being alone with her that she must, surely, have begun to ask herself, "Does he loathe the sight of me?" just as I kept saying to myself, "Does she despise me now? Did it really happen at all? Did she upbraid me, and push me away and draw me towards her again and again?" At last my awe began to defog. Passing her in the little corridor one afternoon, I gripped her hand and said, "Tonight?" She nodded, then to my astonishment burst into tears, and slipped from me into her room.

That night the barriers rose between us at once. I was frightened by her silence into silence. I was repelled, even disgusted, by the stuffiness of the room, the smelly candle, the tousled bed, our humiliating stealth. We gripped one another at every creak, lying rigid to listen. I could have cried for rage when I was alone again. Our public behavior became correspondingly gracious. It was of what I would now call a Byzantine formality, a Mandarin formality. My manner would not have shamed a grand seigneur; hers a princess. There also began between us a series of long, maundering talks about love and marriage which could come to no conclusion, which indeed could hardly have made sense since each of us was trying to instruct the other without exposing the fact that neither of us had anything to reveal.

The fact is only too obvious, we both had within us the same monstrous weapon of destruction. She had imagined too many romantic stories; I had imagined too luxuriantly; both of us had imagined outside ourselves. Fountains and flags and flowers were elsewhere, always elsewhere, under the Himalayas, on the plains of France, an eye-cast across the plain. So, when I asked her about those wonderful winter dances in the Camp and she admitted that she had not yet been to one, the thought had no sequence unfavorable to her because, after all, she *had* met a real lieutenant at the races. Still, her nature's lighthouse was not roving as it used to rove for me at the pier's end. What had attracted me in her had been the flare that said, "This way to the open sea!" I could not avoid seeing that we had both suddenly become dependent: on this cottage (to which we had once turned our backs to look at the lights across the plain), on my uncle, on my father, on the few shillings that they yielded us for pocket money, on the stuffy little timber-lined room with the chamber pot under the bed, and the varnish blistered from the summer heat and one corner of the ceiling damp. The day she clutched me and said, miserably, "Do you love me at all?" I realized that she had become dependent on me. My father came next day. I immediately asked him if I might go to the farm at Newbridge for Christmas, and I went there that very evening.

It was like going out of a dim room into full sunshine. I saw everything clearly. They had all been right about Philly; she was a silly featherhead, full of vaporings and nonsense. I no sooner mentioned the Camp to Noreen than she at once made me see it for what it was. Even during the two months while I had been at the cottage looking across at the Camp, she had cycled across there to three dances and she described them to me fully and simply. There was nothing now about pink cards, and pink pencils and six wineglasses; and when I cried, "But you *told* me!" she only laughed and said she had been making fun of me. That sort of thing might happen in the officers' mess on a special occasion, such as a big dinner dance — she was not certain because she had never been to such an event — but I surely did not think that it was the form at the sergeants' mess? She said that if I wanted badly to take her to a dance there her man would arrange it. And it was clear that she meant this, and that she was now in the habit of going wherever she liked, and in every other way behaving like a grown young woman.

Within an hour I was under her spell again. She seemed to be more beautiful than ever. She was the actuality of all I had imagined Philly to be. But it was not only her beauty that held me now — that mane of sunlight about her head, her full lips the color of a pale tea rose, her body that was just beginning to take on her mother's plump strength. Her real attraction for me now was her blunt matter-of-factness, her willfulness, which produced more and more sighs from my aunt, and frowns from my uncle and growls from Marky, and — a thing I could never have expected — a sudden flood of tears from Nancy on the only occasion that she talked about her.

"But why?" I asked my uncle. "Why?"

The solemnly pitying look he gave me said more than his words:

"Nancy gave up a great deal for that girl. I warned her! But nobody can save a mother from herself."

I discussed it with Marky:

"People have to grow up!" I protested to him. "Noreen must be near twenty."

"I foresaw it," he growled. "And I was right."

None of them understood her. And yet I could sympathize with them. There were times when I almost hated her myself, so greatly did I need her, and so well did she know it, and so ruthlessly did she exact the price of my need, day after day. When she started again to dodge me for days it was solely, I knew well, for the pleasure of making me realize how essential she was to me. I realized it only too well. Within two weeks the pattern of the previous summer began to repeat itself — one day made radiant by her company followed by three without her, so miserably blank by comparison that I could imagine that she had plotted the contrast; appointments made only to be broken, or kept briefly and summarily interrupted. It would not have been so humiliating if she had made it clear to me that I was only a foil or a fill-in for her sergeant; but there were days when she treated me as much more than that, and then, without warning, she would slap me down with those damned three years between us.

The end came after I had spent six whole, empty days cycling around the country desperately searching for her. On the afternoon of that fateful seventh day, just as the first suggestion of twilight was entering the chilly air, I turned down one of those aimless side lanes that lead under the railway towards the level bog. I had come there across the Curragh. After the plain, open as a giant lawn, this hollowed lane, deep under trees slung like hammocks from ditch to ditch, gave me a queer feeling of enclosure, secrecy and remoteness. I had been there once before during the summer, also in search of her, and I had then got exactly the same labyrinthine feeling that I was going underground. That summer day the lane had been a pool of tropical heat, a clot of mingled smells from the overgrown ditches teeming thickly with devil's bread, meadowsweet, loosestrife, cow-eyed daisies, greasy buttercups, purple scabias, great rusty stalks of dock, briars hooped like barbed wire, drooping hawks-beard. This winter evening these flowers and weeds were a damp catacomb of shrunken bones. The fallen leaves were squashy. The arms of the trees were darkly shrunken against the lowering sky. Once a bird scrabbled. Otherwise there was not the least sound. It became almost dark where the lane descended under a stone railway bridge before emerging to end at a wooden gate, gray and worm-eaten, leading out to the bog, now so vague in the half-light that all I saw of it clearly was the occasional eye of a pool catching the last gleams from the watery sky.

She stood with her back to me, leaning over the old gate, gazing out over the bog. She started when she heard my step. My heart was battering, but I managed to say, with a pretense of gaiety:

"Hello, Noreen! Waiting for your beau?"

"And what if I am, nosy?"

"Oho! Nothing at all! Is he letting you down tonight?"

For a second she seemed to bend and slacken, and I

relished the sight. She recovered herself, with a wicked grin.

"You can be my beau tonight. You're not so awful-looking. You'd pass in a crowd, I suppose."

I had leaned idly against the gate. I was wearing my school cap. She took it off, threw it on the ground and brushed back my hair with her palm. A brighter gleam flitted through the clouds. A bog pool glinted greenly behind her shoulder. The smells of the dank vegetation grew thicker. My breath came faster.

"You know, kid, if you did your hair properly . . . Have you no sweetie of your own?"

"Yes!" I said. "Up in Dublin."

"What's she like?"

I could only think of Philly, red-eyed from weeping. I could not talk about that goose to a girl who was going to marry a sergeant who would soon take his commission as an officer and carry her off to England, a married woman. I shook my head dumbly and gazed into her blue eyes.

"Well," she said impatiently, "what does *she* say to you when you walk her out? What do you say to her?" She suddenly dragged my arm behind her waist. "Here! Suppose I was her, what would I be saying to you now?" I shivered at her touch. "Go on!" she mocked.

"I don't think you'd say anything. You'd just look at me."

She looked at me sidewards and upwards from under droopy lids.

"This way?"

"No!" I said furiously. "More like . . . I dunno how! More like a sheep?"

She detached my arm irritably. Then she laughed at me pitilessly. Peremptorily she put my arm back again around her waist.

"You're a very timid courter. Say something to me. As if I was your girl."

I whispered, seeing her cloud of flaxen hair against a pale star:

"You're like an angel, Noreen."

She sighed a happy sigh that was almost a groan. She looked past me up the dark tunnel with heavy eyelids.

" 'Tis like the pictures," she said sleepily. "Go on."

"I could pray to you, Noreen."

"Go on," she murmured, throatily, leaning against me.

"When I see the sun through the window in the priory I think of you, Noreen."

Her eyes were closed. She muttered, as if barely awake:

"Why does nobody talk to me like that?"

"Doesn't your sergeant?"

She opened her eyes wide, blue-sky-wide, and stared at me enormously:

"What window?"

"The window of Mary Magdalen with the long golden hair."

She pushed me away and roared laughing at me; perhaps, I now think, at the pair of us; and was there, I have sometimes wondered, a bitterness in her laughing?

"Honest to God you're a scream!" She quietened and looked seriously at me. "You poor little bastard!" she said. "I don't know what I'm going to do with you."

She really did seem to be considering the problem, so that I felt a great warmth of happiness that she should be thinking kindly about me even if she was a grown woman and even if she still thought I was only a boy. Then she stiffened suddenly, and shoved me away. She had lifted her head like a bird that hears a warning screech from its mate.

"Hop it!" she rapped at me. "Clear out!" — and began to clamber over the gate into the field beyond.

It did not occur to me to disobey. In a daze of shame I went slowly back up the lane to where I had thrown my bicycle against the ditch. Only when I was on the road did I remember my cap, and laying the bicycle aside I went back for it, thinking she had run off into the field beyond the gate. As I came to the bridge I saw them on the other side of the gate, framed by the stone arch, in one another's arms, their mouths locked. Knowledge turned me into a statue. He was not a sergeant. He was not even a private soldier. He was a little buttoned-up lump of a fellow with a coarse cap on his head, peaked upward so that what there was left of salvaged daylight on his little, wizened horse's face made me realize that he could only be a stableman like Marky Fenelon. As I stood there, petrified, his fist clutched her yellow mop and slowly dragged her head backward. Her mouth fell open like the red gullet of a cat.

I slunk into the ditch. Then I crept away up the lane, jumped on my bicycle and rode off like a madman. I was aware of stars through black branches. Behind me, far away, across the plain, a bugle began to unfold its gay elaborate call. As it came and died away I imaged the illusory lights of the Camp flickering in the wind that had silenced the wavering notes, and I thought of that flickering line not as lights but as lies. Yet I did not feel anger, or disgust, I did not feel deceived, or betrayed, or derided. I felt only a hollow in me full of defeat, now and forever after. It was a secret moment. Nobody knew it. Nobody would ever know it. But as I rode through the Main Street of Newbridge, along one side of which the shops were now lighted, and the girls already parading the pavement, and the soldiers coming out of the barracks across the street, in twos and threes, for a night's pleasure, I kept my head lowered over the handle bars, as if I was afraid that some-body would guess my shame in my knowledge of my de-feat.

I had wanted to know what there is to know; to possess life and be its master. The moment I found out that no-body knows, I had exposed myself to myself. I would never do it again. The shame of it was too much to bear. Like everybody else I would pretend for the rest of my life. I would compound; I would invent — poetry, religion, common sense, kindness, good cheer, the sigh, the laugh, the shrug, everything that saves us from having to admit that beauty and goodness exist here only for as long as we create and nourish them by the force of our dreams, that there is nothing outside ourselves apart from our imagin-ings.

I rode home. I was in nice time for supper. My uncle said:

"That's a fine complexion you have. Been cycling?"

"It was a grand day for it!" I smiled. "And a grand night of stars."

He winked at me and began mockingly to hum the barcarole from *Hoffman*.

The next morning as I passed the gate lodge Noreen came out, and with one of her slow, smiling looks, as of a fellow conspirator, she handed me my cap, wet, crumpled and muddy. When I unfolded it I found the silver track of a snail across the lining. I let it fall into the Liffey, where it slowly floated away.

I did not go down there again for a couple of years. By then I was doing medicine at the university. When my Uncle Gerry met me at the station he laughed loudly:

"By Gor, John, I hardly recognized you. They're after making a grand straight fellow out of you. You'd better stop growing up now and start growing out for a change."

As I watched him lumbering into the old tub-trap I said:

"You're after getting a bit on the heavy side yourself, Uncle Gerry."

"Anno Domini!" he said, flicking up the pony, who had also got so fat that he had rubbed the paint off the insides of the shafts.

As we trotted along the road I asked after my aunt, and Marky, and Nancy, and the farm, but what I wanted to get on to as quickly as I decently could was whether he had any tips for the July races. It was not until I was unpacking and came on my father's usual presents for Marky and Nancy that I remembered that Noreen had got married a few months back; for there were two Italian blouses this time, one white blouse for Nancy, and one pale-blue marked *For Noreen,* which I took to be a wedding token. I found Nancy in the kitchen, and I could see no great change in her, apart from a few gray streaks of hair, and that she was getting "right loguey" too. She shouted with delight when she saw me:

"Aha! You're not a child any more! God be with the days when I used to throw you up to the ceiling. But I'm going to kiss you all the same."

And we kissed with double-hearty smacks and laughs. Then I handed over the two blouses with a mock bow.

"With my papa's compliments, madame!"

"They're gorgeous!" she said, laying the two of them side by side. The arm of the blue fell on the arm of the white. Gently she lifted the blue sleeve and let it sink on its own blouse. "I'll post it to her. You heard she went off from me in the heel of the hunt? Aye! She fell in with a soldier here in the barracks and followed him to London. It wouldn't surprise me to hear one of these days that his

regiment was posted overseas, to India, or Africa or Egypt.
Then she'll be gone from me entirely."

She smiled, but it was a sad smile.

"I'm sorry, Nancy. You'll surely miss her."

Her smile went. She said vehemently:

"I will not! There was a time when I'd have laid down
my life for that girl. I don't care no more about her now
than the child unborn." She smiled sadly again. "Ye used
to be great pals at one time."

"Yes," I agreed shortly, and I was glad to turn round
and see Marky darkening the doorway.

We greeted one another warmly. I handed him the
sailor's twist. As we were flattering one another I wondered if I was expected to make the old joke about his getting married to Nancy, but that year I was in love with a
girl at the university and he looked so gray and wizened
and she looked so fat that the joke seemed rather stale and
even a little unseemly. I got him to talk about the July
races, because my uncle had said that he was interested in
a horse called Flyaway, and he started to tell me all about
it.

Suddenly, as we talked, there was a noise behind us,
like a clatter of pigeons rising. It was Nancy rending the
blue blouse from the top to bottom, tearing at it savagely
again and again, her teeth bared, her eyes out on pins.
Marky, undeflected, merely glanced at her and went on
talking in his slow steady voice about Flyaway. We heard
the bang of the range lid. Staring at him, I got the smell of
burning silk. Marky, seeing that I was too dazed to listen,
took me by the arm and, still talking about the horse,
guided me out into the hot sun of the cobbled yard. I
looked back at the kitchen door.

"Never heed her," he said. "She's upset. She feels very
lonely in herself this long time."

"Marky! Did Noreen get into trouble or something?"

"No! She just hoisted her sails, and off with her. It was just as well! Seeing her going off there every night with common fellows around the town, and poor Nancy in that kitchen sitting looking at the fire in the range . . ."

"Wasn't it a pity yourself and Nancy didn't make a match of it?"

He looked at me from under his gray eyebrows and said, quietly:

"And give it to say to everyone that I had another man's child under my roof?"

"What matter?" I cried. "What matter?"

He shook his little bullet head slowly and slowly pronounced judgment:

"It does matter. I heard it said too often that no man nor beast ever loved their young with the fierce love of a woman for her by-child." He tapped me lightly on the arm with the twist tobacco. "If I was you I'd put ten shillings on Flyaway," and he limped away about his affairs.

The natural way back into the house was through the kitchen. Nancy was standing by the range, with the poker in her fist and her graying head to the door. I knew she had heard the lifted latch, but she held her rounded back rigidly against me. I waited. She turned, looked at me and said coldly:

"Well? Do you want something?"

As I looked at her a bugle began to unfold its far-carrying notes from the distant barracks. Then its convoluted call wavered on the changing wind and died away. Did I hear the sparrows chirruping in the walled orchard? Did the ivy at the window rustle? I saw the evening star and the west was already a cold green. Did I smell decaying vegetation? It was the hour when the soldiers would soon be coming out to meet their girls. I made a feeble gesture with my hands, and walked off to another part of the house. I wanted badly to read about Flyaway.

All that happened over forty years ago. I have three children of my own now. One is fourteen, one is nearly sixteen, and the eldest is a few months over eighteen. The middle one is my son. When I happened to look at him the other night across the fire I saw what I felt to be a familiar look in his eyes and all this came back to me. After all, I have now come to the age when memories are meaningful — the age when a man knows that he has lived. The farm has descended to a second cousin, but my family goes down there now and again for a holiday. They tell me that the cottage on the Curragh is completely disappeared, knocked down to make room for a car park. When I talk to them about bugle calls they laugh at me and say: "Daddy! Buglers, and drummer boys, and gun wagons and semaphores and all that sort of thing belong to the time of the Boer War." They say you cannot see the lights of the Camp any more because of the spruce and firs that have been planted there as a shelter belt. But I could always go to the Curragh for the races.

Neither trained horses nor wild horses would drag me down there. The only thing that would tempt me there would be to feel and smell the night over the plain. I daren't do it. I would still see the flickering lights. I would hear the wavering sound of a far-off bugle. And I would know that these things that I could neither see nor hear are the only reality.

Two of a Kind

Maxer Creedon was not drunk, but he was melancholy-drunk, and he knew it and he was afraid of it.

At first he had loved being there in the jammed streets, with everybody who passed him carrying parcels wrapped in green or gold, tied with big red ribbons and fixed with berried holly sprigs. Whenever he bumped into someone, parcels toppled and they both cried "Ooops!" or "Sorree!" and laughed at one another. A star of snow sank nestling into a woman's hair. He smelled pine and balsam. He saw twelve golden angels blaring silently from twelve golden trumpets in Rockefeller Plaza. He pointed out to a cop that when the traffic lights down Park Avenue changed from red to green the row of white Christmas trees away down the line changed color by reflection. The cop was very grateful to him. The haze of light on the tops of the buildings made a halo over Fifth Avenue. It was all just the way he knew it would be, and he slopping down from Halifax in that damned old tanker. Then, suddenly, he swung his right arm in a wild arc of disgust.

"To hell with 'em! To hell with everybody!"

"Ooops! Hoho, there! Sorree!"

He refused to laugh back.

"Poor Creedon!" he said to himself. "All alone in New York, on Christmas-bloody-well-Eve, with nobody to talk to, and nowhere to go only back to the bloody old ship. New York all lit up. Everybody all lit up. Except poor old Creedon."

He began to cry for poor old Creedon. Crying, he reeled through the passing feet. The next thing he knew he was sitting up at the counter of an Eighth Avenue drugstore sucking black coffee, with one eye screwed-up to look out at the changing traffic lights, chuckling happily over a yarn his mother used to tell him long ago about a place called Ballyroche. He had been there only once, nine years ago, for her funeral. Beaming into his coffee cup, or looking out at the changing traffic lights, he went through his favorite yarn about Poor Lily:

"Ah, wisha! Poor Lily! I wonder where is she atall, atall now. Or she dead or alive. It all happened through an Italian who used to be going from one farm to another selling painted statues. Bandello his name was, a handsome black divil o' hell! I never in all my born days saw a more handsome divil. Well, one wet, wild, windy October morning what did she do but creep out of her bed and we all sound asleep and go off with him. Often and often I heard my father say that the last seen of her was standing under the big tree at Ballyroche Cross, sheltering from the rain, at about eight o'clock in the morning. It was Mikey Clancy the postman saw her. 'Yerrah, Lily girl,' says he, 'what are you doing here at this hour of the morning?' 'I'm waiting,' says she, 'for to go into Fareens on the milk cart.' And from that day to this not a sight nor a sound of her no more than if the earth had swallowed her. Except for the one letter from a priest in America to say she was happily married in Brooklyn, New York."

Maxer chuckled again. The yarn always ended up with the count of the years. The last time he heard it the count had reached forty-one. By this year it would have been fifty.

Maxer put down his cup. For the first time in his life it came to him that the yarn was a true story about a real woman. For as long as four traffic-light changes he fumbled with this fact. Then, like a man hearing a fog signal come again and again from an approaching ship, and to last hearing it close at hand, and then seeing an actual if dim shape, wrapped in a cocoon of haze, the great idea revealed itself.

He lumbered down from his stool and went over to the telephones. His lumpish finger began to trace its way down the gray pages among the Brooklyn *Ban*'s. His finger stopped. He read the name aloud. *Bandello, Mrs. Lily.* He found a dime, tinkled it home, and dialed the number slowly. On the third ring he heard an old woman's voice. Knowing that she would be very old and might be deaf, he said very loudly and with the extra-meticulous enunciation of all drunks:

"My name is Matthew Creedon. Only my friends all call me Maxer. I come from Limerick, Ireland. My mother came from the townland of Ballyroche. Are you by any chance my Auntie Lily?"

Her reply was a bark:

"What do you want?"

"Nothing at all! Only I thought, if you are the lady in question, that we might have a bit of an ould gosther. I'm a sailor. Docked this morning in the Hudson."

The voice was still hard and cold:

"Did somebody tell you to call me?"

He began to get cross with her.

"Naw! Just by a fluke I happened to look up your name in the directory. I often heard my mother talking about you. I just felt I'd like to talk to somebody. Being Christmas and all to that. And knowing nobody in New York. But if you don't like the idea, it's okay with me. I don't want to butt in on anybody. Good-by."

"Wait! You're sure nobody sent you?"

"Inspiration sent me! Father Christmas sent me!" (She could take that any way she bloody-well liked!) "Look! It seems to me I'm buttin' in. Let's skip it."

"No. Why don't you come over and see me?"

Suspiciously he said:

"This minute?"

"Right away!"

At the sudden welcome of her voice all his annoyance vanished.

"Sure, Auntie Lily! I'll be right over. But, listen, I sincerely hope you're not thinking I'm buttin' in. Because if you are . . ."

"It was very nice of you to call me, Matty, very nice indeed. I'll be glad to see you."

He hung up, grinning. She was just like his mother — the same old Limerick accent. After fifty years. And the same bossy voice. If she was a day she'd be seventy. She'd be tall, and thin, and handsome, and the real lawdy-daw, doing the grand lady, and under it all she'd be as soft as mountain moss. She'd be tidying the house now like a divil. And giving jaw to ould Bandello. If he was still alive.

He got lost on the subway, so that when he came up it was dark. He paused to have another black coffee. Then he paused to buy a bottle of Jamaica rum as a present for her. And then he had to walk five blocks before he found the house where she lived. The automobiles parked under the lights were all snow-covered. She lived in a brown-stone house with high steps. Six other families also had rooms in it.

The minute he saw her on top of the not brightly lit landing, looking down at him, he saw something he had completely forgotten. She had his mother's height, and slimness, and her wide mouth, but he had forgotten the pale, liquid blue of the eyes and they stopped him dead on the stairs, his hand tight on the banister. At the sight of them he heard the soft wind sighing over the level Limerick plain and his whole body shivered. For miles and miles not a sound but that soughing wind that makes the meadows and the wheat fields flow like water. All over that plain, where a crossroads is an event, where a little, sleepy lake is an excitement. Where their streams are rivers to them. Where their villages are towns. The resting cows look at you out of owls' eyes over the greasy tips of the buttercups. The meadow grass is up to their bellies. Those two pale eyes looking down at him were bits of the pale albino sky stretched tightly over the Shannon plain.

Slowly he climbed up to meet her, but even when they stood side by side she was still able to look down at him, searching his face with her pallid eyes. He knew what she was looking for, and he knew she had found it when she threw her bony arms around his neck and broke into a low, soft wailing just like that Shannon wind.

"Auntie! You're the living image of her!"

On the click of a finger she became bossy and cross with him, hauling him by his two hands into her room:

"You've been drinking! And what delayed you? And I suppose not a scrap of solid food in your stomach since morning?"

He smiled humbly.

"I'm sorry, Auntie. 'Twas just on account of being all alone, you know. And everybody else making whoopee." He hauled out the peace offering of the rum. "Let's have a drink!"

She was fussing all over him immediately.

"You gotta eat something first. Drinking like that all day, I'm ashamed of you! Sit down, boy. Take off your jacket. I got coffee, and cookies, and hamburgers, and a pie, I always lay in a stock for Christmas. All of the neighbors visit me. Everybody knows that Lily Bandello keeps an open house for Christmas, nobody is ever going to say Lily Bandello didn't have a welcome for all her friends and relations at Christmastime . . ."

She bustled in and out of the kitchenette, talking back to him without stop.

It was a big, dusky room, himself looking at himself out of a tall, mirrored wardrobe piled on top with cardboard boxes. There was a divan in one corner as high as a bed, and he guessed that there was a washbasin behind the old peacock-screen. A single bulb hung in the center of the ceiling, in a fluted glass bell with pink frilly edges. The pope over the bed was Leo XIII. The snowflakes kept touching the bare windowpanes like kittens' paws trying to get in. When she began on the questions, he wished he had not come.

"How's Bid?" she called out from the kitchen.

"Bid? My mother? Oh, well, of course, I mean to say . . . My mother? Oh, she's grand, Auntie! Never better. For her age, of course, that is. Fine, fine out! Just like yourself. Only for the touch of the old rheumatism now and again."

"Go on, tell me about all of them. How's Uncle Matty? And how's Cis? When were you down in Ballyroche last? But, sure, it's all changed now I suppose, with electric light and everything up to date? And I suppose the old pony and trap is gone years ago? It was only last night I was thinking of Mikey Clancy the postman." She came in, planking down the plates, an iced Christmas cake, the coffeepot. "Go on! You're telling me nothing."

She stood over him, waiting, her pale eyes wide, her mouth stretched. He said:

"My Uncle Matty? Oh well, of course, now, he's not as young as he was. But I saw him there last year. He was looking fine. Fine out. I'd be inclined to say he'd be a bit stooped. But in great form. For his age, that is."

"Sit in. Eat up. Eat up. Don't mind me. He has a big family now, no doubt?"

"A family? Naturally! There's Tom. And there's Kitty, that's my Aunt Kitty, it *is* Kitty, isn't it, yes, my Auntie Kitty. And . . . God, I can't remember the half of them."

She shoved the hamburgers towards him. She made him pour the coffee and tell her if he liked it. She told him he was a bad reporter.

"Tell me all about the old place!"

He stuffed his mouth to give him time to think.

"They have twenty-one cows. Holsteins. The black and white chaps. And a red barn. And a shelter belt of pines. 'Tis lovely there now to see the wind in the trees, and when the night falls the way the lighthouse starts winking at you, and . . ."

"What lighthouse?" She glared at him. She drew back from him. "Are ye daft? What are you dreaming about? Is it a lighthouse in the middle of the County Limerick?"

"There is a lighthouse! I saw it in the harbor!"

But he suddenly remembered that where he had seen it was in a toyshop on Eighth Avenue, with a farm beyond it and a red barn and small cows, and a train going round and round it all.

"Harbor, Matty? Are ye out of your senses?"

"I saw it with my own two eyes."

Her eyes were like marbles. Suddenly she leaned over like a willow — just the way his mother used to lean over — and laughed and laughed.

"I know what you're talking about now. The lighthouse on the Shannon! Lord save us, how many times did I see it at night from the hill of Ballingarry! But there's no harbor, Matty."

"There's the harbor at Foynes!"

"Oh, for God's sake!" she cried. "That's miles and miles and miles away. 'Tis and twenty miles away! And where could you see any train, day or night, from anywhere at all near Ballyroche?"

They argued it hither and over until she suddenly found that the coffee was gone cold and rushed away with the pot to the kitchen. Even there she kept up the argument, calling out that certainly, you could see Moneygay Castle, and the turn of the River Deel on a fine day, but no train, and then she went on about the steppingstones over the river, and came back babbling about Normoyle's bull that chased them across the dry river, one hot summer's day . . .

He said:

"Auntie! Why the hell did you never write home?"

"Not even once?" she said, with a crooked smile like a bold child.

"Not a sight nor a sound of you from the day you left Ballyroche, as my mother used to say, no more than if the earth swallowed you. You're a nice one!"

"Eat up!" she commanded him, with a little laugh and a tap on his wrist.

"Did you always live here, Auntie Lily?"

She sat down and put her face between her palms with her elbows on the table and looked at him.

"Here? Well, no . . . That is to say, no! My husband and me had a house of our very own over in East Fifty-eighth. He did very well for himself. He was quite a rich man when he died. A big jeweler. When he was killed in an airplane crash five years ago he left me very well off. But sure I didn't need a house of my own and I had lots of friends in Brooklyn, so I came to live here."

"Fine! What more do you want, that is for a lone woman! No family?"

"I have my son. But he's married, to a Pole, they'll be over here first thing tomorrow morning to take me off to spend Christmas with them. They have an apartment on Riverside Drive. He is the manager of a big department store, Macy's on Flatbush Avenue. But tell me about Bid's children. You must have lots of brothers and sisters. Where are you going from here? Back to Ireland? To Limerick? To Ballyroche?"

He laughed.

"Where else would I go? Our next trip we hit the port of London. I'll be back like an arrow to Ballyroche. They'll be delighted to hear I met you. They'll be asking me all sorts of questions about you. Tell me more about your son, Auntie. Has he a family?"

"My son? Well, my son's name is Thomas. His wife's name is Catherine. She is very beautiful. She has means of her own. They are very happy. He is very well off. He's in charge of a big store, Sears Roebuck on Bedford Avenue. Oh, a fine boy. Fine out! As you say. Fine out. He has three children. There's Cissy, and Matty. And . . ."

Her voice faltered. When she closed her eyes he saw how old she was. She rose and from the bottom drawer of a chest of drawers she pulled out a photograph album. She laid it in front of him and sat back opposite him.

"That is my boy."

When he said he was like her she said he was very like his father. Maxer said that he often heard that her husband was a most handsome man.

"Have you a picture of him?"

She drew the picture of her son towards her and looked down at it.

"Tell me more about Ballyroche," she cried.

As he started into a long description of a harvest home he saw her eyes close again, and her breath came more heavily and he felt that she was not hearing a word he said. Then, suddenly, her palm slapped down on the picture of the young man, and he knew that she was not heeding him any more than if he wasn't there. Her fingers closed on the pasteboard. She shied it wildly across the room, where it struck the glass of the window flat on, hesitated and slid to the ground. Maxer saw snowflakes melting as often as they touched the pane. When he looked back at her she was leaning across the table, one white lock down over one eye, her yellow teeth bared.

"You spy!" she spat at him. "You came from *them!* To spy on me!"

"I came from friendliness."

"Or was it for a ha'porth of look-about? Well, you can go back to Ballyroche and tell 'em whatever you like. Tell 'em I'm starving if that'll please 'em, the mean, miserable, lousy set that never gave a damn about me from the day I left 'em. For forty years my own sister, your mother, never wrote one line to say . . ."

"You know damn well she'd have done anything for you if she only knew where you were. Her heart was stuck in you. The two of you were inside one another's pockets. My God, she was forever talking and talking about you. Morning noon and night . . ."

She shouted at him across the table.

"I wrote six letters . . ."

"She never got them."

"I registered two of them."

"Nobody ever got a line from you, or about you, only for the one letter from the priest that married you to say you were well and happy."

"What he wrote was that I was down and out. I saw the letter. I let him send it. That Wop left me flat in this city with my baby. I wrote to everybody — my mother, my father, to Bid after she was your mother and had a home of her own. I had to work every day of my life. I worked to-day. I'll work tomorrow. If you want to know what I do I clean out offices. I worked to bring up my son, and what did he do? Walked out on me with that Polack of his and that was the last I saw of him, or her, or any human being belonging to me until I saw you. Tell them every word of it. They'll love it!"

Maxer got up and went over slowly to the bed for his jacket. As he buttoned it he looked at her glaring at him across the table. Then he looked away from her at the snowflakes feeling the windowpane and dying there. He said, quietly:

"They're all dead. As for Limerick — I haven't been back to Ireland for eight years. When my mum died my father got married again. I ran away to sea when I was sixteen."

He took his cap. When he was at the door he heard a chair fall and then she was at his side, holding his arm, whispering gently to him:

"Don't go away, Matty." Her pallid eyes were flooded. "For God's sake, don't leave me alone with *them* on Christmas Eve!"

Maxer stared at her. Her lips were wavering as if a wind were blowing over them. She had the face of a frightened girl. He threw his cap on the bed and went over and sat down beside it. While he sat there like a big baboon, with his hands between his knees, looking at the snowflakes, she raced into the kitchen to put on the kettle for rum punch. It was a long while before she brought in the two big glasses of punch, with orange sliced in them, and brown sugar like drowned sand at the base of them. When she held them out to him he looked first at them, and then at her, so timid, so pleading, and he began to laugh and laugh — a laugh that he choked by covering his eyes with his hands.

"Damn ye!" he groaned into his hands. "I was better off drunk."

She sat beside him on the bed. He looked up. He took one of the glasses and touched hers with it.

"Here's to poor Lily!" he smiled.

She fondled his free hand.

"Lovie, tell me this one thing and tell me true. Did she really and truly talk about me? Or was that all lies too?"

"She'd be crying rain down when she'd be talking about you. She was always and ever talking about you. She was mad about you."

She sighed a long sigh.

"For years I couldn't understand it. But when my boy left me for that Polack I understood it. I guess Bid had a tough time bringing you all up. And there's no one more hard in all the world than a mother when she's thinking of her own. I'm glad she talked about me. It's better than nothing."

They sat there on the bed talking and talking. She made more punch, and then more, and in the end they finished the bottle between them, talking about everybody either of them had known in or within miles of the County Limerick. They fixed to spend Christmas Day together, and have Christmas dinner downtown, and maybe go to a picture and then come back and talk some more.

Every time Maxer comes to New York he rings her number. He can hardly breathe until he hears her voice saying, "Hello, Matty." They go on the town then and have dinner, always at some place with an Irish name, or a green neon shamrock above the door, and then they go to a movie or a show, and then come back to her room to have a drink and a talk about his last voyage, or the picture post cards he sent her, his latest bits and scraps of news about the Shannon shore. They always get first-class service in restaurants, although Maxer never noticed it until the night a waiter said, "And what's mom having?" at which she gave him a slow wink out of her pale Limerick eyes and a slow, wide, lover's smile.

Angels and Ministers of Grace

"You can dress now, Mr. Neason," the doctor said. He went back slowly to his desk and began to write.

Jacky, still holding his shirt in his palms, looked hard at him and he didn't like the look of him at all.

"Well, Doc?" he got out in a kind of choke between the rise and fall of his Adam's apple. "What's the verdict?"

"The verdict is that your heart is a bit dicky, and your blood pressure is high, but otherwise you're all right."

"A bit dicky?" said Jacky, suddenly crumpling up the shirt in his fists. Still clutching the shirt he sat down. His heart was fluttering like a slack sail. "What do you mean, dicky?"

"Well, without going into technical details, the fact is you've been overdoing it and your old ticker has got a bit tired, that's all. If you go to bed and rest up for a couple of months and take things easy from this on you'll probably live to be a hundred. If you don't it could become very serious."

Jacky forgot his fright.

"Rest? In bed? Sure, flat racing begins next week end!"

"Mr. Neason, you are not going to see a racecourse for another two months. If you do you must get another doctor."

"But, sure, Holy God, I was never in bed for more than four hours any night o' me life! What'll I be doing in bed for two months?"

"You can listen to the radio. And you can read. And, well, you can be listening to the radio. And you can read."

"Read what?"

"Anything not too exciting. Someone once told me that whenever H. G. Wells went on a long journey he used to take a volume of the *Encyclopedia Britannica* with him. I'll come and visit you now and again."

"Can't I come and see you?" Jacky asked feebly.

"It'll be safer the other way," said the doctor, and it was then that Jacky knew he was really bad.

"Can I take e'er a drink?" he asked, now sagging on the ropes.

"A little glass of malt, or a bottle of stout, whenever you feel like it will do you no harm in the world. But keep off women. It takes the blood away from the head."

"I never had much to do with them," said Jacky sourly, putting his head into his shirt.

He went home, took a stiff whisky, told his wife the news and got into bed. When she saw him in bed she began to cry, and she went on crying so long that he had to tell her he wasn't dead yet. At that she buttoned her lips to keep from crying more than ever. She managed to ask him was there anything special he wanted.

"Is there such a thing in the house as an encyclopedia?" he asked.

"Such a thing as a what?"

"An encyclopedia. The doctor said I must read."

She looked sadly at him and the tears came again.

"Poor Jacky," she sobbed, "I never thought I'd see you reduced to this," and she went away to look.

It did not take her long — there were not twenty books in the house; bookmakers don't collect that sort of book — so she went around next door to Noreen Mulvey, the schoolmaster's wife. She was soon back with a big black book with red edges called *A Catholic Dictionary.*

"Where the hell did I buy that?" Jacky asked.

"You didn't. I got it from Noreen Mulvey. She said 'tis as good as an encyclopedia."

Jacky looked gloomily through the funereal volume. He found a green rubber stamp inside the cover. *Saint Jacob's College, Putney Green, Middlesex, London.* There were a lot of queer words in black type, of which the first was *Abbacomites.*

" 'Twill last me out," he said mumpishly and settled himself to read.

The first article informed him that abbacomites were noble abbots, or count abbots, to whom the courts of the time gave abbacies for pecuniary profit. He was further informed that these abbots included not only the sons of nobles but their daughters, and even their wives.

"Nice blackguarding!" Jacky muttered and settled himself more comfortably to read the next article, which was headed *Abbess.* He read the brief paragraph with interest, especially the part that informed him that in the Brigittine Order and in the Order of Fontevrault, where there were monasteries for both nuns and monks side by side, "the monks were bound to obey the abbess of the related monastery."

"My ladies!" he growled sardonically and went on to *Abbots.*

He began to wilt a little here — the article was long and technical — though he rallied at the paragraph describing the bright young abbés, "fluttering around the Court of Versailles," who never so much as saw the abbeys from which they drew their incomes. He weakened again at *Abbreviations* and he nearly gave up at *Abjuration of Heresy,* but he was arrested by the *Abrahamites* because it struck him that these fellows were not far wrong when they declared that "the good God had created men's souls, but the wicked power, or demiurge, had created their bodies." However, at the end of this article there was a reference to a later entry on Manicheanism, of which Jackey read enough to decide that they were a lot of bloody foolahs and that the writer on Abrahamitism had been right to give them hell.

Abraxas bored him. *Absoution* was full of *a*'s, and *b*'s and *c*'s. As for the *Acaeometi* or Sleepless Monks, it was plain that they were another set of born eedjuts. It was then, as he began to ruffle the pages impatiently, that his eye fell on *Adam*. He read this article not only once but three times. When his wife came in with an eggnog she found him leaning back and staring pensively out of the window.

"Come here to me, Eileen," he said, taking the eggnog with an absent hand. "Did it ever occur to you that Adam and Eve made nothing at all of going around in their pelts?"

"Everyone knows that," she said, tucking in the bed-clothes.

"What I mean is did it ever occur to you that they didn't mind one bit?"

"I suppose the poor things were innocent until the devil tempted them."

He cocked his head cutely at her.

"I'll go so far with you," he agreed. "But did it ever occur to you to ask how did the devil manage it if they were all that innocent?"

"Why wouldn't he?" she scoffed. "Isn't it the innocent ones that always fall?"

"Fair enough," he agreed again, and then in the smug voice of a chess player saying "Checkmate," he said: "But

what you're forgettin' is that this was in the Garden of
Eden where sin didn't exist."

"The devil invented it," she said hurriedly.

"Heresy!" he pronounced and tapped the book. "I'm after
reading it here under *Abrahamites*."

"Will you have chops for your supper?" she asked.

He nodded without interest.

"It only stands to reason," he pointed out. "You can't
tempt a man who is so innocent he doesn't mind seeing a
woman going around in her pelt."

"But what about the apple?" she cried.

"Aha! But what *was* the apple?"

" 'Twas just an apple. Anyway it was something they
weren't allowed to have," she declared with all the vehe-
mence of a woman who knows that she does not understand what she is saying and must therefore say it as
emphatically as she can. But Jacky was, by now, beyond
arguing along these lines. He said loftily that the Council
of Trent left the matter entirely open. She whisked her
head in the air, and at the door she turned to remark with
proper feminine unfairness, and irrelevance, that it would
be better for him to be saying his prayers.

By suppertime he had moved farther on. Conquering all
the territory that he touched, he learned much that he had
not previously even thought it possible to know about the
subject of *Adultery*. It was an article with cross references
to *Marriage* and *Affinity*. When Eileen came back with the
supper tray, bearing two fine chops and a glass of Guinness
with a one-inch froth on it, she again found him looking
thoughtfully out of the window. As she laid the tray on his
unheeding lap he said:

"Did you know that a man can't marry his own mother-
in-law?"

"Your mother-in-law," she informed him coldly, "is in her grave this seven years. And when she was alive you hadn't as much as a good word to throw her no more than to the cat."

"I am not," he told her with a nice and infuriating blend of courtesy and condescension, "discussing your mother. It is a question of canon law."

Her breath went up her nose like the whistle of a train.

"Eat your chops while they're hot," she said, and went out with prim hips.

Milo Mulvey called in about ten o'clock to offer his condolences to the patient. Eileen told him to save his sympathy because her hero (her own term) was full of buck and guff. She led him upstairs and while he sat on a cane-bottomed chair by the bed she leaned over the end of it. Milo adopted the false-jolly manner of all visitors to sick-rooms.

"Well, Jacky my ould tar," he cried jovially, "so this is what slow horses and fast women did to you?" — with a wink at Eileen to take the harm out of it.

"Milo!" Jacky addressed him seriously. "Do you really believe that a thousand angels can stand on the point of a needle?"

Milo looked at him, and then he looked a question at Eileen.

"He's that way all day," she said. " 'Tis all on account of that book you gave him."

"Is that mine?" Milo asked, leaning over to glance at the somber volume. "Where did you get it?"

"I borrowed it from Noreen today. Worse luck. The professor here said he wanted to read something."

"You poor man," Milo said, "I'll bring you around half a dozen detective stories."

"Thanks," said Jacky, "but I don't want them. This is
the most interesting book I ever read in my life. Barring
that book of famous crimes you lent me last year when I
had the flu. But do you — and this is a serious question
now mind you — do you really and truly believe that a
thousand angels can stand on the point of a needle?"

"You're very interested in religion all of a sudden,"
Milo said suspiciously.

"For a man," Eileen agreed dryly, "who wasn't to church,
chapel or meeting for the last five years."

Jacky leaned out of bed and tapped Milo's knee.

"Milo! Will you tell me how the hell's blazes could even
one angel stand on the point of a needle, let alone a thousand of 'em?"

"Answer the professor," Eileen said wearily to Milo.

"Well," Milo began, a bit embarrassed and not sure he
was not being chaffed by the two of them, "if you are serious about this the answer is, of course, that angels are pure
spirits. I mean they can pass through walls and floors and
ceilings. I mean they have neither length, nor breadth, nor
depth. I mean they are pure intelligences."

"What you mean," Eileen said flatly, "is that angels have
no legs."

"Well," Milo conceded unwillingly, "that is more or less
what it comes to."

"The professor," she said in a long sigh, "is now about to
ask you how they can stand if they have no legs."

Milo laughed easily. He turned to Jacky. He was a man
who loved explaining things, which was why he was a
teacher.

"That's very simple, Jacky. Let me explain it to you.
You see, when you say 'stand' you don't really mean 'stand.'
You mustn't take these things literally. You know very well,
for instance, that when you say 'going up to heaven' or

'going down to hell,' you don't mean 'up' and 'down' the
way we mean upstairs and downstairs. It's the same with
everything else. I mean you don't think God has whiskers,
do you? You follow me?"

He found himself faltering. Jacky was looking at him
rather coldly, something like the way a boss-gangster
might look at one of his gang who is explaining volubly
how he happened to be seen coming out of the headquar-
ters of the police precinct the previous night at half past
eleven arm in arm with the district prosecutor. Milo turned
to Eileen:

"*You* understand me, Eileen, don't you? I mean it's impossible for us to as much as talk of things of this kind
without forming misleading pictures of them. But, of
course," with a fluent wave of his hand, "that doesn't mean
that our pictures bear any relation to actuality. I mean we
don't think that angels have actual wings and all to that,
do we?"

He laughed cajolingly, anticipating her answering smile
of approval.

She did not smile. She looked sadly at him. Then she
looked at Jacky.

"Go on, professor!"

"All the same, Milo," Jacky said, "I believe it is a fact
that the angels can commit sin?"

"Well, they certainly did once," Milo agreed, but his
eyes were beginning to get shifty. "The fallen angels and
all that. Milton," he added absently. "*Paradise Lost.*"

"And what," Jacky asked with a polite interest, "do you
suppose they did it with? Having no legs and so on?"

"With their minds!" said Milo wildly.

"I see," said Jacky. "With their minds."

There was a long pause. Eileen came to the rescue with

"Would you like a bottle of stout, Milo?", very much like a boxer's second at the end of the tenth round saying to a man whose only wish on God's earth is that he had never come into the ring, "Would ye care for a small brandy?"

Milo said that he would, yes, thanks, he would, thanks very much, take a, in fact, yes a bottle of stout if she had one handy. As she leaned up and went for the stout she heard Milo acceding to her hero that a lot of these things are difficult to our mortal understanding, and Jacky magnanimously agreeing that he could see that, and:

"Take the Garden of Eden, now, for example!"

When she came back with the tray she found the two heads together, going word for word through a page of the black book. She observed that Milo looked much less jovial than when he sailed into the room a quarter of an hour before.

Milo did not call in again until several nights later. He had not been in the bedroom for ten minutes, chatting about this and that, when the doorbell rang. Eileen went down and came back accompanied by Father Milvey. She showed his Reverence in, and when he and Milo greeted one another with as much astonishment as if they had not met for six months, she looked over at Jacky, caught his eye and gave him a moth-wink out of a porcelain face. (The parish joke about the firm of Mulvey and Milvey had moss on it.) Father Milvey was a tidy little man, always as neat as a cuff straight from the laundry; and he might have been thought of as a tidy, cheerful little man if he had not had a slight squint which gave him a somewhat distant look. He greeted the patient with the usual sickroom cordiality. Eileen went downstairs for the bottle of whisky, and after she had come back and helped them all round, and helped herself, she took up her usual position leaning over the end of the bed, waiting for his Reverence to mention the Garden of Eden. He did it very simply.

"Yerrah, what's the big book, Jacky? Oh? I hope it's not one of those American things, all written in words of one syllable and as full of pictures as if the Vatican was in Hollywood. Well, the Lord knows 'tis high time you took a bit of interest in something else besides horses."

Jacky fended him off just as simply. He pushed the book aside with a casual:

"Ach, it passes the time, Father."

There was a short silence. Then Milo made the approach direct.

"He had a bit of difficulty there the other night, Father, with the Garden of Eden. As a matter of fact it stumped myself."

"Oho, is that so?" said the little priest with a cheerful laugh. "Nothing like beginning at the beginning, is there? And what was that now?" he asked Jacky, and Eileen saw his hand moving slowly to his pocket, and protruding therefrom the corner of a pale-green pamphlet. She foresaw the look of surprise, could already hear the words, "extraordinary coincidence . . ."

"Ah, nothing much," said Jacky.

"What was it, though?"

"Hell!" said Jacky.

Father Milvey's eyes strayed towards Milo's. The look plainly meant: "I thought you said angels?" His hand came back to his glass. He smiled at Jacky.

"No better subject for a man in your position, Jacky. Did you ever hear the one about the old lad who was dying, and the priest said, 'Now, Michael, you renounce the devil, don't you?' Do you know what the old chap said? 'Ah, wisha, Father,' says he, in a very troubled sort of

voice, 'I don't think this is any time for me to be antago-
nizing *anybody!*' " He let the laughter pass, and then he
said easily: "Well, what about hell?"

"Fire!" said Jacky. "I don't believe a word of it."

His Reverence's face darkened. Help for the humble was
one thing, the proud were another matter altogether. He
adopted a sarcastic tone.

"I think," he said, "the old man I was just telling you
about was a little more prudent in his approach to the question of hell-fire."

Jacky took umbrage at his tone.

"There's no such a thing as hell-fire," he said roundly.

"Oh, well, of course, Mr. Neason, if you want to go
against the general consensus of theological opinion! What
do you choose, in your wisdom, to make, for example, of
those words: 'Depart from me ye accursed into everlasting
fire prepared for the devil and his angels?' "

"Angels?" asked Jacky, lifting his eyebrows.

Milo intervened hastily:

"I think, Father, what was troubling Jacky there was the
question of angels being pure spirits."

"What of it?"

Jacky, a man of infinite delicacy, lowered his eyes to his
glass.

"I must say I fail to see your difficulty," his Reverence
pursued, and put out his palm when Milo restlessly started
to intervene again. "No, Milo! I *like* to hear these lay theo-
logians talking."

"Ach, 'tis nothing at all, Father," Jacky said shyly. "I'm
sure 'tis a very simple thing if I only understood it. Only.
Well. Pure spirits, you see? And real fire? I mean, could
they, so to speak, feel it?"

"Tshah!" cried Father Milvey. "Suarez . . ." He halted.
It was a long time since he had read his Suarez. "Origen,"

he began. He stopped again. It was even longer since he
had read his Origen. He wavered for a moment or two, and
then he became a nice little man again. He expanded into
a benevolent smile. "Wisha, tell me, Jacky, why does all
this interest you anyway?"

"It just passes the time, Father."

Father Milvey laughed.

"You know, you remind me of a man — this is a good
one, I only heard it the other day . . ."

Eileen leaned up. She knew that the rest of the visit
would pass off swimmingly.

It was four days before Milo called in again. Jacky
thought he looked a bit dark under the eyes, but he
decided not to remark on it. Anyway Milo did not give him
time; he threw his hat on the bed, sat on the chair, leaned
forward with his two hands on his knees, and stared at
Jacky with a fierce intensity. Normally, Milo was a rotund,
assured sort of man; his tiny mouth, like a child whistling,
pursed complacently; a man as resolutely tidy-minded as
the row of three pens in his breast pocket, each with a little
colored dot to indicate the color of the ink. He did not look
like that at all tonight. Jacky looked at his furrowed brow
and the deep, forked lines from his nose to his button-
mouth, and wondered could he be on a batter.

"Jacky!" he said harshly. "All this about hell!"

"Yerrah," Jacky waved airily, "that's only chicken feed.
You explained all that to me. 'Tis all figurative." To change
the subject, he leaned over and tapped Milo's taut knee.
"But, come here to me, Milo, did it ever occur to you that
the antipopes . . ."

Milo choked. He sat back.

"Look!" he almost sobbed. "First it was angels. Then it
was fallen angels. Then it was hell. Now it's antipopes.

Will ye, for God's sake, keep to one thing. I'm bothered to blazes about this question of hell."

"Don't give it a thought," Jacky soothed him. "You mustn't take these things too literally. I mean fire and flame and all that!"

"But Father Milvey says, and he's been reading it up, that you must take it literally. My God, 'tis the cornerstone of Christianity. All the eschatological conceptions of the postexilic writings . . ."

"You're thinking too much about these things," Jacky said crossly.

"Thinking?" Milo gasped and his round eyes flamed bloodshot. "I've done nothing for four days and four nights but think about it! My head is addled with thinking!"

"I'll tell you my idea about all that," Jacky confided. "I believe there's a hell there all right but there's no one in it."

"That's what Father Conroy says!"

"Who's he?"

Milo's voice became sullen. He explained unwillingly:

"He's the Jesuit that Father Milvey's consulting about it. But Father Saturninus says . . ."

"I never heard of him. Where'd you dig *him* up?"

"He's the Capuchin who's conducting the mission this week in Saint Gabriel's. The three of them are at it every night inside in the presbytery. You know very well that the sermon on hell is the linchpin of every mission. Fire coming out of the noses of the damned, fire out of their ears, fire out of their eyeballs, their hands up for one half-cup of cold water — you know the line! Mind you, not that I approve of it! But it always gets the hard chaws, it gets the fellows that nobody else and nothing else can get. Well, Father Saturninus says all this talk and discussion has him off his stroke. Think of it! Every night people waiting for the sermon on hell and Saturninus climbing up in the pulpit knowing they're waiting for it, and knowing he won't be able to do it. Of course, he could easily talk about hell as a lonely, miserable, desolate place where everybody was always groaning and moaning for the sight of heaven and having no hope of ever seeing it, but you know as well as I do that a hell without fire, and lots and lots of it, isn't worth a tinker's curse to anybody."

"Well," said Jacky impatiently, "I don't see how I can help you. If you want to believe in fire and brimstone . . ."

Milo grasped his wrist. His voice became a whisper.

"Jacky," he whispered. "I don't believe one single bloody word of it."

"Then what are you worrying about?"

"I'm worrying because I *can't* believe in it! I was happy as long as I *did* believe in it! I *want* to believe in it!"

Jacky threw his hands up in total disgust.

"But, don't you see, Jacky, if you don't believe in hell you don't believe in divils, and if you don't believe in divils you don't believe in the Garden of Eden." His voice sank to a frightened whisper again. He seized Jacky by the arm. Jacky drew back his chin into his chest, and crushed back into the pillows to get away from the two wild bullet eyes coming closer and closer to him. "Jacky!" whsipered Milo. "What *was* the apple?"

"A figure of speech!"

Milo dashed his arm away, jumped to his feet, gripped his head in his hands and uttered a hollow and unlikely "Ha! Ha! Ha!" in three descending notes like a stage villain. His voice became quite normal and casual.

"Can *you* eat a figure of speech?" he asked very politely.

"There was no eatin'. That was another figure of speech, like the angels that have no legs."

"You mean, I presume," Milo asked, with a gentle and

courteous smile, and a delicate shrug of his Rugby-player's shoulders, "that Adam had no mouth?"

"Adam was a figure of speech," Jacky said stolidly.

"I'm going mad!" Milo screamed, so loud that Jacky had one leg out of bed to call Eileen before Milo subsided as quickly and utterly as he had soared. He smiled wanly. "Sorry, old boy," he said in the stiff-upper-lip voice of an old Bedalian on the Amazon who has rudely trod on the tail of an anaconda. "A bit on edge these days. Bad show. I only wish I could see the end of it. The worst of it is Father Milvey says it's all my fault keeping such books in the house. And lending them to you. I wish to God I never gave you that book! I wish to God I never laid eyes on it!"

Jacky fished it out of the eiderdown and handed it to him.

"Take it," he said. "I'm sick of it. 'Tis all full of 'This one says' and 'That one says.' Have you er'er an ould detective story?"

"But, Jackey! About *hell?*"

"Forget it!" said Jacky. "Eileen!" he roared. "Bring up the bottle of whisky."

"No thanks," said Milo, getting up gloomily and putting the obscure volume under his arm. "Father Milvey is coming around to my place tonight and I'll have to have a jar with him." He looked down miserably at Jacky. "You're looking fine!"

"Why wouldn't I, and I living like a lord?"

" 'Tis well for you," Milo grumbled sourly, and went out slowly.

After a while Eileen came upstairs to him bearing the whisky bottle, two glasses and a big red book.

"What's that book?" he asked suspiciously.

"Milo gave it to me for you. 'Tis *The Arabian Nights.*

He said not to let Father Milvey see it. Some of the pictures in it will raise your blood pressure."

Jacky grunted. He was watching her pouring out the liquor.

"Come here to me, Eileen," he said, his eye fixed thoughtfully on the glass. "Did it ever, by any chance, occur to you that . . ."

"What is it now?" she asked threateningly, withholding the glass from him.

"I was only going to say," he went on humbly, "did it ever occur to you that the bottom of a whisky bottle is much too near the top?"

She gave him one of those coldly affectionate looks of which only wives are capable, added a half-inch to his glass, and handed it over to him.

"You ould savage," she said fondly, and began to tuck him in for the night. To show her approval of him she left the bottle by his side.

Left to himself he opened the big red book. He savored it. He began to relish it. He was soon enjoying it. He snuggled into his pillow and, with one hand for the page and one for his glass, he entered the Thousand and One Nights. Thanks be to God, here at least there were lots and lots of legs. Towards midnight he gently let the blind roll up to see what sort of a night it was. His eye fell on the light streaming out from Milo Mulvey's sitting room across the grass of his back garden: the theological session in full swing. He raised his eyes to the night sky. It was a fine, sweet, open-faced night in May. A star among the many stars beamed at him. There are more things in heaven . . . With renewed relish he returned to the Grand Vizier's daughter. His glass was full.

One Night in Turin

One robin-singing, cloud-racing, wet-grassed Monday morning last April, Walter Hunter came down to breakfast as usual at half past eight — nice time to let him drive at his ease to his office in Cork city for ten, a gentlemanly hour — picked up his neatly folded *Irish Times* from the hall table and roared into the rear of the house, "Deviled kidneys forward, Mrs. Canty." He glanced at the headlines as he passed out onto his lawn. The glass door flashed sunlight, greenery, and cloudland about his head. He surveyed with pleasure the host of daffodils on his dew-wet fields stretching down to the low tide, the cloud-castles over the harbor, but on crackling the paper wide open forgot all about them, breakfast, his office and work. The first entry in the *Social and Personal* column read: "The Countess Maria Rinaldi has arrived in Dublin and is staying for a few days at the Russell Hotel." He lifted his head, looked here, there and everywhere among the racing clouds as if he had suddenly heard the twittering of a flock of duck, turned and walked quickly back into his study to telephone her. Just as his fist closed on the receiver he paused, like a stopped film. For one minute he was immobile. In that minute he remembered the seven occasions — especially the first and last — on which he had seen her since she left Ireland, sixteen years ago.

The first occasion was now part of his blood stream. It had occurred in 'Forty-six. He had gone with Betsy Cot-

man to Cervinia, ostensibly for the skiing. It was his first
trip abroad since the war, that event whose prolongation
so insensibly aged us all. Two years before it began he had
gone back to study at the King's Inns, belatedly finishing
his law studies, feeling himself still a student among students. By 'Forty-six he was coming down the straight to
forty; still handsome, with a few interesting flecks of gray
on his temples, in perfect physical trim, having already
put half of a good life behind him — he knew it all, he
would tell you, with a gay wave of his long fingers — and
with the clearest intention of holding on to his good fortune as long as possible. Cervinia, however, had not been
entirely a success. Betsy had stayed with him for only three
days — she then had to hurry on to St. Moritz to establish
herself there before her husband came out — but he had
seen her go with relief. In those three days and nights he
had discovered that she had no interest in anything that
she could not manhandle as a form of healthy sport. Her
whole life seemed like a long and rich dinner where every
course was a repetition of the pleasure of the last course
under a different name. Whether she was skiing, toboggan-
ing, mountain climbing, figure skating, or making love,
she never altered her tone one jot, never abated her voice
by as much as a quarter tone. She had leaped like a chamois
from the snow to the bed, from the bed to the snow, oblivious of the chasms that yawned between her inexhaustible
store of hearty Anglo-Saxon good cheer and his Irish sensi-
bilities. He waved her good-by between a sigh of satisfaction and a breath of nausea, and returned deep-breathing
to the pure white mountains. He got in four days of mid-
dling-to-good skiing, and then the threatened wet snow fell.
He came down into Torino to eke out there the last forty-
eight hours of his brief holiday. (His father had died during the war, he was in charge of the family business of

Hunter and Hunter, so that all his escapes now had to be intense and brief.)

He was delighted to be alone in snow-covered Turin. Never having stayed before in any Lombard or Swiss city in bad weather, he discovered for the first time the merits of those northern arcades which both allow and tempt one to pass sociably and in comfort from café to café. He was excited by the contrast between these crowded cafés and the sense of isolation that he got from the warnings of the white heaps of bomb rubble, the silent white ruins of crumbled houses, the brown desolation of the swollen Po, the great white, empty squares bluishly lit at night by lean streaks of light from lower-floor windows. As he wandered about, he recalled the many trestle bridges over which his train from Paris had so cautiously crawled. He felt like a pioneer postwar explorer. How wonderful, he thought, it could be to be completely cut off here for a couple of months. He would pass his days in one café after another, hot and steamy, smelling of coffee and *nazionales*. He would make the acquaintance of a few intelligent and interesting men in whose company he would forget all about his stupid and slightly humiliating adventure with that fool of a woman.

His first night was not a success. He spent it in a big, chattering café in the Piazza Carlo Felice. There was no trouble at all about making acquaintances — tourists were still few enough to be interesting novelties in 'Forty-six. But he got buttonholed by one old, bearded character who talked with the same inexhaustible and unprofitable energy about war and politics in Italy as Betsy had about hunting and fishing in England and Ireland. Also, that night he had an unpleasant dream. He dreamed of being squashed (right across his smooth, soft belly) by some great collapsing weight — like an ant one crushed underfoot. He awoke and lit the light to drive away the image. Would he feel terrible agony? Or would it be immediate death? Would he, dead or alive or unconscious, wriggle galvanically like a fly in a candle-flame for a second? He thought of brutal writers and painters who have painted such cruel things. Faulkner? Describing a man burned in a plane crash. Hemingway, describing a man thumbing out another man's eye and then biting off the dangling eyeball. Algren. Why do they do it? Exorcising, or indulging their egos?

There was not a sound from the street. The snow silenced every outer noise. We drag our ego with us through life, chained to it, in its power, not it in ours. We are free of it, or seem to be free of it, only in rare hours — relaxed by the achievement of climbing a mountain peak, elevated by the speed of a dangerous ski run, in the quiet hour after love, calmed by the wonder of some splendid view, asleep, when slightly drunk, listening to music. Where had he heard or read of a man of the most strict behavior who came within an inch of being killed by a falling beam, who said to himself, "I was as good as killed! Well, then, my past is finished," and proceeded to spend the rest of his life in the pursuit of pleasure? He thought, for no apparent reason, of Betsy Cotman — and groaned with displeasure. When he awoke, his light was still lighted. The grimness of his dream remained with him for several hours — an unpleasant wash of gray color across the sunny morning.

He spent the forenoon shopping: a trifle for his cook, she was worth the attention; a trifle for his secretary, poor thing; an expensive pair of gold earrings for Betsy, these affairs had to be finished off in style. The afternoon and evening he spent in three different cafés, where, again, the talk was easy, amiable, and unimportant. He dined well, went to an American movie, and on the way home was accosted at a dark corner by a young man who tried to sell him a fake Parker 51 fountain pen. Walter took the pen in his hand, it came apart immediately and the young man burst into tears. Walter took him to a bar for a drink and the young man revealed his misery. He had spent his only five hundred lire on ten of these fake pens, expecting to re-sell them for two thousand five-hundred. He laid them on the marble table — they were all defective. He had been cruelly defrauded. Walter watched him take one apart and fiddle with it, passionately, despairingly. When the top half of the casing would not screw into the bottom half, he burst into tears once more. Walter gave him a thousand lire and they parted like old friends. But as Walter went out he looked back. The young man was again tearing at the pen. He never forgot that image of the young man's despairing efforts to undo his disaster. He often told his friends about it. "It brought," he would say, "the whole war, the whole of Turin, down to the point of a pen."

His second, and last, day passed just as pleasantly. He went to see the alleged Veil of Veronica in the cathedral. He was not impressed. At lunch he met a man with one arm, an unrepentant Fascist who knew, as a certain fact, that Mussolini had never been shot — it was his double who had been shot — was hiding in Switzerland and would return again to lead a resurgent Italy. He listened to some more vague talk in two more cafés, content to sit on there, slowly filling up his cooling-tank with the ice water of their new-found patriotic ideals and his own moral resolutions. By the time he had again dined and wined himself well he was in an entirely pleasant state of mental and emotional euphoria. It was at this moment that his great adventure began.

His eye fell on a poster — they were playing *La Sonnam-bula* that night at the opera. He hastened around to the theater, managed to procure a ticket, took his seat just

as the lights dimmed, and within minutes he was leaning forward, rigid with excitement. Molly O'Sullivan had
walked on to the stage as the miller's daughter, Amina. At
once there grew in him the strangest and sweetest sense of
secret complicity with her life — the only man in the whole
theater who had known her as a girl, indeed almost as a
child, in Ireland. This feeling was so sweet and strong that
he immediately resolved never to tell anybody at home in
Ireland that he had been in the theater that night. He resolved not even to send his card around to her. If he did,
he would have to meet her in the company of other admirers behind the scenes, where she would simply become
public property — the wonderful new soprano who had
been discovered in a wayside *taverna* in the wilds of Ireland. She would no longer be the charming young girl on
whom he first laid eyes behind the counter of old Katy
O'Sullivan's pub in Coomagara — a pub well known to all
late travelers between Cork and Kinsale for being open
at all hours, for bad whiskey, poor measure, and the blond
charms of the daughter of the house — good-looking in a
saucy way, he had thought her the first time he saw her, as
vain as a peacock, an outrageous flirt, almost too obviously
nobody's fool, but, just as obviously, as innocent and (he
had quoted Yeats to himself on their first encounter) "as
ignorant as the dawn." In her crowded dressing room she
would neither be that enchanting apparition emerging, in
pure white, under pale, cold, greeny moonlight to mourn
her lost love, nor the young girl he used to secretly admire
in Dublin during the couple of years after her discovery,
whom he used to ambush casually in dusty teashops, in
the distempered corridors of the Academy of Music, or
walking with her fellow students across Saint Stephen's
Green, past the old bandstand, the great beds of gerani-
ums, and the statue of George the Third facing the humped

bridge over the ponds. He left the theater as furtively as a kidnapper. He would write to her when he got home. He would come out again in the summer and confess everything to her.

When he got back home to Hunterscourt he bought recordings of the opera, and, that winter, whenever he put them on for his friends he felt again the secret bond that he had formed with her in Turin, so that if one of his guests asked some such simple question as, "Is this by Verdi?" or, "Wally, is this the opera with the song that Joyce's ould father used to love?" he would not correct them, he would not hear them, he would say, in the detached voice of the president of the Cork Grand Opera Society, "There's a rather nice little aria coming up now." Then, hearing once more the "*Ah, non credea mirarti*" or the "*Ah, non giunge,*" he would lean back in his armchair by the fire to see her again, gleaming like a snow maiden under a canopy of light and music; or see himself, after the performance, half stunned by delight and wonder, sipping brandy after brandy in a mirrored café by the railway station, with his packed bags and his oiled skis on the floor beside him, waiting, long after the crowd had thinned away, for the Rome-Paris Express to pass at two in the morning, drunkenly watching the wet snowflakes melting on the panes, sinking heavily into the palms outside, floating in a white fuzz around the cloudy electric lights, and now and again a soft thunder rolling dully down from the mountains along the tawny valley of the swollen Po. He had no clear recollection of the journey home. He remembered only her gleaming image, the music, the falling snow, the heavy, silent streets.

One thing about her soon began to disturb him. At first her image came obediently when he called her. Presently he ceased to control her. Now it was she who ambushed him. Her image became so merged with his own being that any least disturbance in any corner of his senses could awaken her from her coiled sleep, until he came to realize that he had had his greatest illusion of power over his thoughts of her when he was most subject to them. He did not write to her. He did not go to Italy that summer. It was as if he feared to meet her. After that it even seemed to him that she spied on him. Whenever the thought of her visited him among his legal cronies, or among his Bohemian-theatrical friends up in Dublin, he became terrified that some day he would talk to them of her, and he went among them no more. More than that — his affairs with women became infrequent, casual and coarse. "The worse the better," he said to himself — though not excusing himself, for it was his self-boast that he never deceived himself about anything.

Being a lawyer accustomed to examining other people's motives, he naturally spent many hours trying to understand why he kept on postponing an avowal of his passion for her. After long consideration, he decided that she was like certain lights that can be discerned only by not looking straight at them — a dim star, a remote airport beacon in a fog, a lamp in a distant cottage window. She represented something in himself that he could only approach obliquely and slowly. "After all, you don't change your politics or your religion all of a sudden," he caught himself saying aloud to himself one night. Besides, he knew that nobody really lives entirely by what he professes. She was his illogical goddess. He remembered a Catholic friend of his who was always good-humoredly teasing him for being a Protestant — "next door to an atheist" — meaning a man for whom nothing existed beyond the earth, the body and the understanding. Yet this pious man, he found out, always carried a four-leafed clover in his cigarette case as a luck charm.

"Against what, in your good God's name?" Walter had asked him with a grin. "Destiny!" said his friend, with a fierce glare.

He did not blame his friend for teasing him. It must have seemed to many that he had indeed lived all his life by the law of passionate pleasure. He had loved sport — hunting, shooting, fishing. Hunterscourt, his father's and his grandfather's home before him, was ideal for any man who enjoyed the open-air life: an old Georgian house (originally the dower house of Lord Boyne's estate across the fields) situated twelve and a quarter miles out of town on a hundred and fifty acres of mixed land ranging from rich alluvial soil down to the kind of reedy-quaggy fields that you find so often along the lower Lee. On any fine morning, before driving into his office in his Mercedes-Benz, he could hack about for an hour on his little demesne, or wander with his gun, or if it is high tide sail down the creek into Cork Harbor to cast a line, or swim in his pelt, completely unobserved, or merely lie on his back gazing up at the harbor sky, vast, always cloud-packed, faintly mobile. The house had half a dozen modern loose-boxes. He had plenty of friends glad to come down for a few days' sailing or for rough-shooting on another hundred acres that he had rented and preserved around the hills of Fermoy. As for other pleasures, where could a man be better situated than within a bare twenty minutes of a modern airport with planes for Dublin, and from that onward to any city on the Continent that he cares to choose? He had several times taken off from Cork after a leisurely lunch on Friday, enjoyed two crowded days in Paris, and on Monday morning walked into Hunter and Hunter's on the South Mall, and hung up his bowler hat and his umbrella with as staid and contented a "Good morning, Miss O" and a "Morning, Mr. Dooley" as if he had spent the week end reading *Sense and Sensibility*.

What his good friend did not realize, of course, was that it palls. After forty, it begins to pall. He had not realized it himself until that night in Turin. Those hesitations ever since, all those oblique and sidelong efforts to see the dim star, the cottage window, the airport beacon in the fog, were — he now knew — his efforts to understand what it was that he had desired and not found in the hunt, the shoot, on the wind-pocked sea, all these casual women.

Having settled on one explanation for his prolonged hesitations and his frightened secrecy about her, he at once decided on two more — that the real reasons he was being cautious were (a) that he was so much older than she and (b) that he really did not know anything about her as a woman. (His great motto about women had always been a minatory, "They change, you know, they change!") Accordingly, he kept on making and remaking decisions about her, until he suddenly realized that he had, as it were overnight, become two years older, and so had she, which made both his reasons still more cogent. He thereupon wrote several letters to her — and did not send them. He booked train and plane reservations to go out and meet her, and did not go. One morning his paper announced that she had married Count Giorgio Rinaldi, a landowner with some undefined industrial interests near Bergamo. He wrote to her at once, to congratulate her, assuring her that this was what she both deserved and needed. His second and third encounters with her occurred soon after.

These were the years when his holidays happened to take him to the Dolomites: he visited her and Giorgio in their home outside Bergamo. He made these visits nervously, and after much hesitation. They established only that she had ceased to be an opera singer, that she was living in the grand manner, and that she was a beautiful woman of skill and taste, with a high, marble-white fore-

head, delicately veined, big gray eyes, globular as a Peki-
nese's, a poreless skin, exquisitely carved lips and a great
pile of braided, blonde hair — a rich, mature beauty,
with an Italian-style figure. Anybody who had not known
her as Molly O'Sullivan of Coomagara could easily have
thought she had always been a *contessa*. She was, he reckoned, thirty or thirty-one. He was nearly forty-three.

The next winter he met them twice in Milan; once for
dinner before the opera at Crispi's; the second time, after
the opera, when the three of them walked, chatting happily
arm in arm, across the foggy piazza and through the arcade for late supper at Savini's. It was a gay night, as gay
and warm in feeling as the little red table lamps and the
chatter of the crowded arcade. She was completely real to
him that night, both as Molly O'Sullivan and as the Contessa Rinaldi.

The next summer, when he happened to be motoring
along the lakes from Berne to Venice, he called on them one
afternoon where they were in *villeggiatura* in a small cottage above Lecco. High up there it was cool. They drank
cold white wine. The lake below was a dark blue. They
could see the snowy Alps. He noted, with satisfaction, that
the marriage was a childless one.

It was on their last, entirely unplanned, meeting, seven
months ago, in Rome, that his swift thoughts converged
as he stood immobile over the black telephone. That night,
he very nearly told her his secret about the snowy night in
Turin. Unfortunately, neither the place nor the occasion
encouraged the exchange of memories, least of all that kind
of memory. She had come to Rome because Giorgio had
come there to consult a specialist. He had met her so unex-
pectedly, with such a shock of delight, that for a moment
he could not talk to her, at a diplomatic cocktail party in
the Palazzo Farnese. Since she could not dine with him —

she had to go back to the nursing home to dine with Giorgio
— he persuaded her to meet him afterwards at Doney's for
a nightcap.

She came, late, so that his nerves were all on edge before she entered, dressed as she had been at the Embassy,
in a costume of raw silk the color of alder-flowers, not
much lighter in hue than her hair, and even her wide
floppy hat of openwork straw was covered in cream lace,
its white brim fringed about her sun-tanned face. She
looked so lovely, though so troubled, that he regretted he
had not selected a more secluded place than a Via Veneto
café. He was relieved that he had at least chosen to meet
her indoors at Doney's, where it is usually quiet enough
in warm weather, when the crowds prefer to sit outside,
three deep on the sidewalk under the colored canopies.
By ill luck, just as they sat to a table in a quiet corner indoors, a sudden September cloudburst fell on the city, and
at once the hundreds of gossipers on the pavement came
rushing indoors, laughing noisily at the unexpected disaster, carrying their drinks, obtruding everywhere in the
salon, with waiters racing in and out, holding chairs aloft
as if they were going to brain everybody. Even so, as he
listened to her telling him Giorgio's symptoms — she feared
the usual malignancy — he was sure he could detect certain
resonances, conveyed by the tone of her voice rather than
by the words, certain undertones not connected with her
fears for his bodily health, taut, nervous, accentuated
perhaps by the rattling rain, the low peals of summer
thunder, the gabbling crowd.

He stared at her, crouching, shaking his head in sad
condolence, smiling with affectionate pity across the brown
table, his bat's ears sharpened by his amorous feeling for
her. He became aware that her beauty, tonight, was not
only rich but sad, and, on an instant, he was transfixed by

the true meaning of her melancholy and moritural loveliness. It came to him when the brilliant lights of the chandeliers suddenly dimmed as if they had all been lowered into the sea, a loud peal of thunder reverberated over the rain-torn city, and the *salon* sent up a laughing, cheering scream of mock fright. In that second he saw her exactly as he had seen her seven years before in the pallid moonlight of *The Sleepwalker,* her eyelids drooping not for Rinaldi but for herself. He cunningly threw out a casual remark about the happiness of Bergamo and coupled it with that gay night in Milan when they all three had hurried arm in arm across the foggy piazza to the warmth of Savini's and the cheery vulgarity of French champagne with the ritual *risotto al salto.* She replied to his remark — he had trembled while he waited for her reply — with an all but imperceptible lifting of one shoulder. In that instant he knew that they had ceased to love.

He had been about to win all her trust when the dimmed lights rose again into a full white blaze and the crowd cheered and applauded as if they were at the end of an opera. He had turned and glared at the laughing gabblers as if to shout, "Silence in the court!" When he turned back he found that she was looking intensely at a young couple beside them, bantering one another loudly and happily, hands clasped across the table. Walter gazed, just as enviously, at her exquisitely curved mouth. As if she felt his look she turned swiftly to him, said brightly in a comic, stage-Irish brogue, "Well, is there e'er a dhrop left in our ould bottle o' fizz?" — and the sole propitious moment of the night was gone.

The storm passed over. The night was warm and bland again. The *salon* emptied. They talked for a while about what they called their past lives. Since they had not talked alone for many years, this was his first real opportunity to

observe how her mind had developed in the meantime. As
they talked she became so heated about a couple of remembered (or imagined) insults from her early critics that he
began at first to fear that she was a blend — not unfamiliar
and very displeasing to him — of the willful and the unworldly. She conveyed a sense of something wanton, something wild, forcibly bearing off a nature entirely simple
and innocent like a strong tide carrying a child's boat out
to sea. It fitted in with his first impression of her long ago,
in that pub at Coomagara, as a proud, flirtatious girl,
"ignorant as the dawn"; as it fitted also with his vision of
her at the opera, a sleepwalking snow maiden wrapped in
a canopy of cold light and passionate music. Not that he
would have minded her being willful or unworldly; but he
was always disturbed by the willful who are also unworldly.
He had met them only too often in his business — the
Irish are a litigious people — unpersuadable, passionate
men and women coming into his office, saying fiercely,
"I want justice!" or "I'll fight to my last penny for my
rights!" As he saw things, the unworldly man (unless he
had abandoned the willful life struggle altogether, like the
priest or the professor) was no man. He was unsexed, weak
and womanish. Likewise, the unworldly woman (unless
she had left the world to become a nun) was no woman.
She was a childlike, retarded, silly creature of no interest
to any grown man. In fact to him the words man, woman,
willful and unworldly were mutually destructive. He could
not even enjoy novels about unworldly women living in the
active world, not even satires about them, such as Jane
Austen wrote; they were not grown up, they were not nu-
bile, they were not playing their proper role in life.

They strolled arm in arm to the Piazza Barberini. By this
time he was more eager than ever to be certain whether she
had or had not been unhappy with Rinaldi; a thousand

times more eager to find out why she had been unhappy —
if she had been; ten thousand times still more eager to
know if she had been worldly enough to have taken a lover.
The lights shivered over the fountaining spume of Triton.
A *carrozza* and two taxis stood waiting. He simply had to
dare ask the question uppermost in his mind:

"Molly, we've known one another for so long you won't
be angry at my asking you something. You have been unhappy with Rinaldi, haven't you?"

She did not answer. She shook her head so slowly that
she might have meant anything by it, such as, "Who is not
unhappy?" or "How impossible it is to talk of such things
now!" It might have been meant as a rebuff. It was a poor
evasion, since by not denying it she had virtually admitted
it. Nevertheless, a slight doubt remained. He tried another
approach:

"Is it very lively in Bergamo?"

"It is intensely boring. The place is so small. So conserva-
tive. So clannish. You can imagine it. You live in a small
city yourself, or is it a large town? We both know what
Cork city is like. Rainy, too, like Bergamo. If Milan were not
so near Bergamo, it would be unbearable. They all go to
Milan for their pleasures as people from Cork go to Dublin, or to London. Or," she smiled, looking crookedly at
him, "to Rome. At first this used to upset me. It seemed so
cowardly. Why on earth, I used to ask myself, don't people
lead whatever life they want to lead? Rinaldi explained to
me that it is universal practice not to. Half the tourists, he
pointed out to me, are provincials on the loose. We have
some American business acquaintances. One of them is a
very intelligent and amusing man from the Middle West.
He once said to us that all over the United States, even in
the most puritanical parts, certain cities are specially pro-
tected or preserved for this purpose. He once described

to us what night life is like in Kansas City. I was fascinated and appalled."

He pressed her arm.

"In so boring a city you must be pestered by would-be lovers?"

"Bergamo is full of feelings of honor."

Her answers enchanted him: intelligent, evasive, delicately ambiguous, a true woman of the world out of another age.

Her taxi draw up. He lifted her hand to his mustache.

"I'll see you in the spring!" he cried. "If not sooner."

Since then he had written to her several times. She had told him in her Christmas letter that Rinaldi had died. He had written his condolences. In March he had asked if he might visit her in April.

Two birds, black as the telephone, darted past his window in a flurry of wings and love song. He slowly lifted the receiver, saying to himself, "If she will lunch with me today, I will tell her about that night in Turin. If the fact that I have kept that secret all these years doesn't convince her . . ." He finished it aloud: "I'll be back here tonight."

2

All the way up to Dublin he made and remade plans. He would blurt out nothing. There were still one or two things about her that he must probe. Had she really been unhappy with Rinaldi? Had he been unhappy with her? If so, whose fault was it? That possible lover? Would she want to marry again? He counted her years in Italy. Bergamo. Milan. Rome. Venice. What would she now think of Cork city, of Hunterscourt! It could be as fine a setting for her, by God, as Castle Boyne next door to him. At once he abandoned the idea — nobody must know until everything was certain. If he failed, they would call him an old fool, an old goat, an old ram.

He passed thirty or forty miles seeing her in his home. She would sing every year, at their opera. Sometimes it lasted a full week. She could be the queen of the whole county. Of the whole country! They would travel, following the opera to Covent Garden, Paris, Salzburg, the Scala, the San Carlo, Rome, the Fenice. Then, just as he was imagining them walking arm in arm from the Hotel Danieli across the Piazza San Marco into the lanes leading to the Fenice, there jumped into his head a remark made to him by a kind friend in Cork only two weeks before in the Yacht Club — it was actually young Boyne, Lord Boyne's eldest brat — "You know what it is, Wally? You must be by now the oldest established bachelor in the whole of the County Cork! And, by God, you're *still* eligible." At the sting of that *still*, he almost doubled his speed. Then he slackened it. He was soothed by the recollection of the image he had formed of her at that midnight farewell by the fountain of Triton: a woman of the world out of another age.

Across the table she looked as beautiful and elegant as ever — those lamplike eyes, the corn-fair hair, poreless skin, tinted eyelids, pallid lipstick, paler nails, Via Monte Napoleone frock (she admitted it), tinkling wrist. But where he had expected a *contessa,* he found a young stu-

dent. She behaved exactly as she had the first time he
had seen her in Dublin in her student days, crossing the
Green from the Academy with two other girls, laughing
aloud, white-mouthed, red-lipped, tongue-showing like a
cat. When he mentioned it now, she laughed in the same
way, and her strong arm across the lunch table grasped
his hand like a boy.

"Isn't it wonderful?" she cried, so loudly that people
nearby turned to frown, and remained looking, transfixed
by her beauty.

"What," he asked hopefully, "is wonderful?"

"My being here, of course! Back where my life began.
I've done so much, I've traveled, I've made so many friends,
I've been flattered and feted wherever I've gone, and nothing, nothing, nothing has been so marvelous as this coming
back, not just to Ireland only, not just only to Dublin —
though it's so beauuuuutiful! — but to this very hotel, on
this same old Green, that I used to cross every day on my
way to the Academy. Do you remember when we were
young, Walter? We used to think this hotel was only for the
big nobs? Now I have a suite in it. My bathroom is in pale
green, even down to the bidet. My bath is sunk in the floor
like a Roman bath. Me! Molly O'Sullivan!" She laughed
at her folly. "What are you doing in Dublin, Walter?"

"I'm on a secret mission."

"Big business?" — with big eyes.

The waiter, bringing the champagne bottle to show, gave
him time to command himself.

"If you must know, I'm here because of a woman."

She again seized his hand in her boyish grip.

"Who is she? Do I know her? Tell me at once. What fun!
Are you thinking of marrying? It's not too late."

"I'm not young," he confessed wryly. "I'm forty-six."

"If the heart is young! How long has this been going on?"

"For quite a number of years."

She drew back.

"Then it can't be secret? You said, 'a *secret* mission.' "

Caught by her great eyes, he felt his chest tighten. He was on the point of confessing everything to her when the bottle popped. While the waiter poured for him to taste he formulated a new plan. When the waiter had poured for both of them, and gone, he said:

"Molly! I'll go to confession to you. The reason I rang you was because I want your help. I'm going to spend three days on my secret mission. Within these three days I'm going to decide. Advise me. It's true you are much younger than I am. But you have been married and I have not. Am I being foolish? Marriage is no joke at forty-six."

He observed her intently. Her eyes sank slowly to her plate. With her fork she began slowly to divide the orange salmon. Was she guessing? Then she lifted her glass, and her eyes were full of kindness.

"Success!" she smiled. "Tell me about your ladylove."

"She is about your age. Your coloring, too. She was married. Her husband died. I'd have married her long ago if I hadn't let her slip through my fingers when I was young. Besides, she was engaged, and I didn't want to upset her."

He believed he had always been drawn to her, but that she had been always dedicated. He was merely interpreting her vocation as a form of engagement. If he were to explain his meaning to her in this way she would understand immediately. He went on telling her of his long devotion and his long restraint.

"And so," he finished, "when she became free again I found all my old feelings lighting up as warm as ever after all these years."

"I would never," she said warmly, "have thought it

of you, Walter. I had always thought of you as more interested in your career than in anything or anybody else. Tell me more about her."

His ladylove — so she had called her — lived in Ireland until she was about twenty-one. She had taken a degree in arts at Dublin University. Then she had gone abroad. To Spain. As a governess. After a year of this an uncle died and left her a small legacy. She immediately went to London. To a school of acting. During the war she fell in with one of the Free French. A young aristocrat. Interested in play production. For four years she did all sorts of acting, including provincial repertory. She twice got small parts in the West End, but she never really succeeded on the London stage, probably because, immediately the war ended, she married her Frenchman. They went to live abroad. In Bordeaux.

She was staring out at the Green. He added that there had been no children. She went on looking out at the Green, slowly turning her champagne glass. He said he had an idea that the marriage had not been entirely happy.

"I," she said, without turning her head, and stopped.

He leaned forward.

"I," she said, "you might say, could have made Rome. Even," a little less assuredly, "Naples?" Still less assuredly, "Even Milan? Instead, I married. I am back," and she stopped again. She finished, speaking with sudden bitterness, "where I began. She sounds very interesting," she said without interest. "I suppose it was because of her you didn't take any interest in me when I was at the Academy. What is her name?"

"I will tell you her name on Wednesday night, my last night, if you will dine with me."

She smiled warmly, laying her hand on the back of his hand.

"Very well. But if you have not succeeded in your great adventure it won't be a very happy occasion? And if you have succeeded it won't be with *me* you'll be wanting to dine?"

He laid his free palm on the back of her hand. She castled her free palm on the back of his.

"That," he said, "is all you know! I'll be so happy if I succeed that there's nobody on earth I'll want to tell everything to sooner than you — where we will live, and what we will be doing for the rest of our lives."

She gave him a curious look.

"Tell me where you live. I ought to know your house from the old days. Isn't it called Hunterscourt? Where exactly is it?"

He told her all about his house. She asked him so many questions about the life he led, about the people around him, about his neighbors and friends that he wondered if she had already guessed what he was after. Her questions were a bewildering blend of ignorance and shrewdness, as when she asked, with a knowing air, if all fillies ran faster than colts, or, "Is it a fact that the Shannon is the widest river in the whole world?" But then, when he would be feeling completely dismayed by her folly, he would find himself being asked some coldly sensible question about current land values in Cork County. Was she a grown woman only by fits and starts? They talked for so long that he suddenly noticed that they were the only two people in the restaurant. He immediately became terrified — he had established nothing, found out nothing, asked nothing to the point of his quest, and here she was collecting her gloves. He said wildly:

"But you should see Cork again yourself. It is really a little Bergamo. With the hills, too! But not the antiquities. Or the sun. We haven't the same food. Or the wine.

Why don't you pay us a visit? I have a whole big house eating its head off."

"As a matter of fact I was half thinking of visiting some friends there."

He felt a twinge of dismay. He knew nobody in County Cork who could have met her since she became famous.

"Who are these friends?" he asked crossly.

"Old Lord Boyne."

He felt the bite of jealousy. He had gone across his fields to Castle Boyne twice to dine and had had the Boynes back twice to dinner at Hunterscourt: they had talked of Italy, but never mentioned the Rinaldis. Old Boyne's crumbling demesne wall shut out the world.

"I did not know," he said coldly, "that you knew the Boynes."

"We met them last year. We were all staying at the Villa d'Este. In May."

"In May."

How childish! In May, before the tourists came. Then you retired to the mountains, then you might look at the sea, turn up later in Venice, go to Egypt if you had the money, then try the skiing, then return to Milan for the gossip and the season. It was a little common of her, really. He drew the lunch to an abrupt close.

As she walked ahead of him past the cocktail lounge she glanced in and casually waved to somebody in there. As he passed he also looked into its artificial dusk. It was young Boyne, his long legs hooped up at the counter. They raised friendly hands in mutual salute. He got the unpleasant feeling of being spied on. In the foyer she thanked him for the wonderful lunch and half turned to the stairs. In sudden despair he held her hand.

"How long are you staying here?"

"Three days."

"Let's dine tonight!" he begged. "You haven't given me any advice at all!"

"*Magari!*"

She had a dinner date. Lunch tomorrow? She was going out of town for lunch tomorrow. He had to be content with dinner tomorrow night — his second day otherwise wasted.

"I know so little about you," he said plaintively, still holding her hand, looking at her. "Have you relatives out of town? I mean, that you are lunching with tomorrow?"

"We are lunching at Killeen Castle."

"We?" he smiled, apprehensively.

"I'm going with young George Boyne, he wants to buy a filly from the Sassoon stables." She shook his hand. "*A domani!*" she beamed at him. "And, *caro*, best of luck in your secret mission. *Ciaou!*"

Two steps up, she laid her hand on the newel post, turned gracefully and to his amazement winked at him. As if his secret love were some sort of jolly joke! He followed her with lifting eyes and chin. He frowned at the faint ridge of corset across her taut Italianate bottom. The calves of a peasant. He called to her just as she was about to disappear at the turn of the stairs:

"Molly! I'm being around town. Is there any little thing I can do for you?"

She glowed. Yes, there was a small thing. To collect a package from the cleaners, who, she laughed, do express cleaning but not express delivery.

"It will be a pleasure."

He turned away, bewildered. Definitely not quite a woman, much more than a girl, yet with all the mature beauty of a desirable woman. He wondered how Rinaldi had handled her. Not easily, he guessed, remembering having read somewhere (he had wondered how the fel-

low knew it) that no women in the world are more passionate than the Irish and less erotic. The thought explained her. He smiled happily and slyly as he moved
towards the desk where the hotel register still lay open
after the last arrival. She was still unspoiled. And unde-
spoiled. His smile vanished as his eye fell on George
Boyne's signature. He stood in the doorway, glaring mood-
ily at the sunlit Green. He turned back and, from the desk,
rang her cleaners.

"Yes!" a girlish voice cried, gleefully and proudly.
"Countess Rinaldi's dresses are all ready."

Dresses? Yes. Two frocks, one costume and an over-
coat. He became scarlet at the idea of her expecting him to
carry all that load of stuff through the city's streets. He
gave the doorman half crown, bade him have the parcel
collected, and went across the street into the Green, whirl-
ing his stick with annoyance. Really, he thought, the woman
is completely juvenile.

Very different, *very* different, to what she had led him to
expect.

3

She stood by the window, the lace curtain in her hand,
and watched him cross the street and enter the Green,
gaily twirling his walking stick. Dear Walter, always fancy-
ing himself the lady-killer. I sometimes wonder is he a

homosexual, with all that pomade, and the wavy hair, and
the smell of *eau verte,* and the tight waist, and the flower
in the buttonhole and the dandy's walking stick.

It's wonderful to be back. A lunch like that now with an
Italian and he'd be playing footy with you all the time,
pressing your knee, paying you sugary compliments. All
poor old Walter wants to do is to talk about himself and
amuse you. Just the same, even one little compliment would
be appreciated. Such as, I heard about your singing, or, I
hope you're going to sing for us in Ireland. I said, So that's
why you didn't take any interest in me when I was at the
Academy, and he just opened his mouth like a fish. But
that is the one great drawback in Ireland — they never
ask you about yourself. So you're back? they say. That is
achievement enough for them.

She drew a deep, slow breath as if she were about to
break into song.

And God knows they are right to have a good opinion of
themselves, the kindest people on earth. Look at him there
now trotting off so nicely to collect my things for me.

He can't be serious about that woman. Or did he make
her up? There never was any such a girl in Dublin in my
time or I'd have heard of her. It's another one of his jokes,
like Cork being a little Bergamo, with the hills, but without the sun, or the monuments, or the food, or the drink. I
must tell that one to George. He'd have made it sound perfect if he'd said, And without the mothers, and the grandmothers, and the aunts, and the great-aunts, and the great-
grandmothers. But he couldn't be serious, he'd be crazy,
he's bald at the top, fifty if he's a day, and when we were
at the Academy we thought he was ages. I well remember
that first morning I saw him on the Green, with Lil Boy-
lan and Judy Helen. Judy nudged me and said, Here's the
college Don Juan, so I put on a great laugh, pretending not

to see him at all, doing the innocent young girl up from the country. His eyes nearly fell out of his head. God help me, I didn't need to do much pretending. Sweet seventeen, and now I'm twice as old and with not much more sense. If it's crazy for him, what about me?

He went out of sight among the trees. She let the curtain fall. She looked at herself in the full-length mirror between the windows. She lifted her chin, pulled in her waist and jerked up the corners of her lips.

Thirty-four, and still thinking of *l'amore?* The last word of the famous first act. I never sang Mimi. I haven't the range. It would be another story if I was an actress like his friend. They can go on forever, like men, but not a singer, or not at my age.

She slowly ran her palm up under her chin to see the crepe gather.

That Fratella woman who cracked in the top C in Foggia! The way they whistled at her! Imagine having to take to the road again. Bari. Taranto. Reggio. Catania. What a night! *Carmen.* The rain and the wind howling in from the sea, and an old chipped enamel bucket plonking like a double bass in the corner of the dressing room at every drop from the ceiling. I got six encores.

She smoothed down her hips, turned to laugh sideways at herself, jacket open, hands on hips, wrenched-back shoulders, tilted chin. *L'amour est l'enfant de Bohème qui n'a jamais, jamais connu de loi. Si tu ne m'aime pas je t'aime, prends garde à toi.*

I suppose I ought to be out in that lovely green sun.

What is keeping him down there? I don't even know for certain how old he is. He says twenty-five but all young men add it on, or grow beards like Aldiberti — but he says it sells his *tessuti* better. All I get out of him is compliments, flattery galore, the old Irish plamaus, but always

dodging off like a trout just when I think, He's going to ask
me now. Like a little fox. Sly. A darling, dear, furry little
fox, with a long brush. Giorgio! He's only a boy. If he was
an Italian I'd know he was only after the one thing. Dear
God, if he is, what must he think of me?

She jangled her wrist loudly. She went to the window.
Two girls, carrying books, passed along the rails. She shook
her head over them littley-bittley. She chuckled fondly as
they passed away gossiping.

Was I innocent when I went to Italy? I was a total fool.
And *still* am! Like saying, I'm back where I began. Letting
myself down opposite him. And even then he didn't pay
me a compliment. Does that damn bar never close? *Sono la
Contessa Maria Maddalena Rinaldi.* And what is it to the
Contessa Rinaldi to be the Countess of Boyne? And anyway old Boyne will live to be a hundred. A little Bergamo?
I want a big Bergamo, Rome, Paris, London, New York.
God in heaven, do I want the same thing all over again? I
was mad to have come. It was God sent him, there's no
fool like an old fool, I must be mad, I'll finish off the whole
thing, I'll have nothing more to do with him, when that
telephone rings I'll just say, very, very quietly, a bit sad,
to make it real, there's no need to hurt him, I'll say, Giorgio,
a terrible thing has happened, I have just received a telegram from Coomagara where my grandfather lies seriously
ill.

The telephone buzzed.

I'm independent of him. I could always live in Dublin.
They'd jump at me for the Dublin Grand Opera. I could
sing for the Rathmines and Rathgar. I could sing on the
radio.

The telephone buzzed.

It couldn't be Aldiberti. He doesn't know where I'm staying. But if I say Coomagara he'll say, I'll drive you down. I.

The telephone buzzed.

She put her handkerchief to her mouth and ran to the window, and then ran back to the telephone, and snatched it up.

"Giorgio! What on earth are you doing down there? No, *caro,* you will *not* come up here. Yes, yes, and I might too if it were Milano again. But this isn't Milano. I will meet you in the foyer. Oh! I have had such an amusing lunch. I must tell you all about it. Such an amusing lunch! Such fun!"

4

Halfway across the Green he stopped dead. He felt that triple pain of emptiness, inertia and frustration which man calls loneliness. He crossed over to the Club. The bar was closed, the library was empty, the billiard table lay under a gray shroud. He walked slowly, killing time, twirling his stick, down the quays to Farquharson and Murphy's about a conveyance that, he knew, could as well be settled in a month's time by a post card. He walked back, slowly, across the Liffey, over Capel Street bridge, along the quays, along Grafton Street, into Knowles's, where he ordered two dozen red roses to be sent at once to her room. On the card he wrote: *Carissima, Red Roses for Thee.* He walked slowly on to Prost's, where he had a shampoo and a hot towel. He walked out to the Shelbourne. He had a word with Leo at the door. He had a word with Christy

O'Connor at the bar, and a prolonged Tio Pepe. He then decided to have tea in the lounge. He stood at the door and recognized three old regulars. His breath stopped. She was seated in a corner, laughing gaily with young Boyne. He withdrew quickly and went out. Outside, he bought the *Evening Mail*. He saw, with a groan, that the Rathmines and Rathgar were once again, yet once again, doing *The Mikado* at the Gaiety. There was not a damn thing that he wanted to see, not even a movie. He looked aimlessly all about him. He walked to the hotel. He undressed. He went to bed.

He awoke at six. He had a bath. He shaved. He changed. He went down to the front door. He selected Davy Byrne's for his *apéritif* and strolled, with pleasant anticipation, across the Green. The public part of the bar was full of what he called up-from-the-countrys, men and women with felt hats and paper parcels. He was about to persist into the rear lounge when he thought, though he was not certain of it, that he saw, through the ornamental wrought-iron gate, young Boyne's poll, and thought, again uncertainly, that the poll turned and a cold eye glimpsed him. He turned to go, and then, because he had to be certain, turned again and entered through the gate into the lounge bar. There was nobody sitting at the table by the gate. On the small black-topped table he saw two glasses, one half filled. She had not told him who she was dining with. He went swiftly through the bar and out through the rear door, and by the side lane back to the street. He saw nobody there whom he knew. He walked across the street to the Bailey. There he found a red beard talking about vintage cars in a loud haw-haw voice to a black R.A.F. mustache a foot wide. He went down to the Buttery. It was crowded, but there were a few two-splits-behind and a few fast fillies, so he sat up at the bar. He had a word with George and a prolonged Tio Pepe. He was afraid to dine at any city restaurant, so he walked back to the hotel. He got out the Mercedes and drove out of town to the Yacht Club. He parked, reserved a table, and went for a stroll along the East Pier.

He always liked the force of that stony white arm curved against the ponderous sea. Dublin smoked faintly to the west, low-lying as an encampment, sharp-edged as a saw, pensive as Sunday. Great pink clouds lay like overblown roses strewn along the bruise-blue horizon. Inch by inch the calm evening began to fade into a dusk the color of cigarette smoke. Some townspeople, lured by the calm weather, were walking on the pier, taking the air, inspecting one another. A few early yachts, anchored to their reflections, pointed their noses eastward — the town's best weather vanes. For a few moments he paused to watch the gulls soaring and sinking about the funnel of the mailboat steaming gently at its pier. At first he passed many strollers, in pairs and fours, chatting companionably, but they became fewer the farther out he walked towards the pier's end with its lighthouse lantern blank and unrevolving.

Gradually he felt the wide sky, the wide bay and the oncoming dusk begin to envelop and isolate him. Now there were no strollers at all. The white tower and the glass of the many-windowed lantern rose coldly above him. When he looked back he saw a few lighted windows along the front. He barely made out the seagulls circling above the mailboat, blue blobs, but he did not hear their cries. The tall windows of his club were greenly lit. Behind the town the Dublin mountains rolled, empty and opaque, as if he were looking at them through smoked glass. Suddenly a yellow finger of light touched the dusty water of the harbor, moved across it, and then the electric string of lamps along the front and down the pier were lit. He climbed the stone steps up the side of the sea wall and went out through the embrasure. There was the night sea, the cold east wind, the sullen wash and slop of waves, one star.

How wonderful it would be now to have her, here, by his side, about to dine with him, hostess of a big dinner party in the club, at the head of the table, admired, glancing lovingly down its length at him. They would have lots of parties. How wonderful it would be to turn from this sea and wind and find her coming towards him now through the dusk, his phantom, seagull-white, smiling with winged lips. They would walk back along the stony arm, her soft arm in his. They would dine in the club, alone, make plans for travel, talk about opera, return to the city, not needing anybody, together, alone. The chilly wind said, But she isn't. Away out in the darkness the Kish lightship blinked. The chill wind said, Aren't you a fool to dream like this? What would one of your clients, what would Farquharson or Murphy think of you? He replied, self-mocking, This is another department, and remembered that somebody (and with a start he remembered that it had been old Lord Boyne) once said to him, We are rational about everything except our passions and our children. The wind said, It is cold. His shiver admitted it. He descended the steps and walked swiftly back along the dark and empty monolith. It was like some big public building closing for the night.

He was glad to see a fire alight in the club. His table was marked *Reserved,* unnecessarily — it was early in the season for diners. There was nobody in the silent dining room with its empty white tables; its portraits of bearded commodores, its enormous Victorian seascapes bloomed like grapes. Once a man's head appeared around

the door, said a cheery good night, and vanished. He heard
the voice of a young man bantering the waitress in the
kitchen, and her repeated laughter. He had often seen
her smile, never heard her laugh. Once he thought how,
more than once during the day, he had had half a notion
to throw up the whole thing and go back to Cork. Not now!
He drank off his claret with determination. Tomorrow night
he would put her to the test. Finally.

The lighthouse swept at intervals. He prolonged his
brandy, carefully shaping the words he would say to her.
His blood thickened. The dark thickened. He dared not
look at his watch. There were no hands on its face. The
mailboat hooted before departure. Only nine? He called
for a cigar. He ordered another brandy and took it into
the reading room so that the waitress could be finished
with him. He sat in the empty reading room, on the long
leather-covered settee, facing the harbor and the beam that
slowly circled and recircled the compass of the night.
Slowly his courage oozed. She was at this moment dining
with George Boyne.

He surrendered, went to his Mercedes, and drove into
the bright city, and through it, and out of it, for home,
driven by the furies of his own folly, contempt for his in-
decision, worked-up hate, bitter pride, cruel reason. It was
after two when he pulled up at the gate to Hunterscourt.
The house was dark. Here, together, when dark came, after
dinner, they would not hear a sound unless it would be
Mrs. Canty in the kitchen rattling cutlery, or the fire put-
tering at their feet; later they might hear cows munching,
or a plane facing out over the sea; latest of all, lying together in the darkness, they would hear nothing at all.

He turned and drove hell-for-leather back to Dublin,
chasing his shivering headlights, passing sleeping cottages,

dark villages, echoing through empty towns. He would insist on seeing her at breakfast.

5

George was laughing at her across the small, red table lamp. Over its upthrown light his handsome young face, pointed like a fox, his wide, mocking mouth, his madcap eyes, gleamed like a teen-age Mephistopheles.

"Tell him at breakfast," he said. "Why keep the poor old fathead in misery until dinner?"

When he drew back she had to peer around the red lamp to see him. Usually when he was in this crazy mood she wanted to devour him the way a mother wants to devour a baby. Through her tears she was aware how his air of wickedness suited him.

"I can't believe it," she protested. "Old Walter!"

"He's not as old as all that," he said crossly. "Be realistic. He's not much older than you than you are than me. He is still considered one of the most eligible bachelors in County Cork."

"But I assure you — he never uttered one word to me about marriage."

"Molly! For the last time! He told you he was in love with an Irishwoman. Whom he met when he was a student. Who studied abroad. Who went on the stage, married a foreigner, lived abroad, is now a widow, has your coloring, is about your age. And he said he is in Dublin to try his fortune with her. Isn't that enough? Without the two dozen red roses — and the *carissima?* What more do you want? Unless," his voice hardened as he again leaned over the little lamp-glow and peered at her with suspicion, "you've been making it up. *Pour encourager les autres?*"

She leaned back, twisting her rings, surveying his under-lighted face.

Earlier they had strolled around the Green, had tea at the Shelbourne, strolled again, just barely dodged him in Davy Byrne's. They dined happily at Jammet's until the wine and the brandy began to go to his head and he had begun groping under the table.

"I don't want that, Giorgio!"

"Liar!"

"Well, not only that!"

"Then what else do you want? A title?"

"I have a title."

"Haw-haw! Wop title!"

She made him apologize; he fell into a dark mood, and would not talk. Embarrassed by the waiters' glances — she suspected that they were not unacquainted with his moods — she had quietly proposed that they bring the evening to an end, whereupon he suddenly became plaintive and begged her not to break off on this note. So they drove, in his car, out of the city up into the hills to the turn of the road at Killakee from which all Dublin lies below, a half-dish of lights encircling the dark bay. Far away a lighthouse slowly circled.

She had been afraid there might be more demands for caresses here. Instead, when she withdrew to her end of the seat, leaning against the window, looking down at the lighted plain, he withdrew to his corner. He did not even once touch her hand. They were silent for a long time.

Then he said, reverting to an earlier run of talk at the Shelbourne:

"Tell me more about your lunch today. It fascinates me. What exactly, tell me again, did old Hunter say about this woman of his?"

She humored him, let him lead her through the whole conversation, back and forth, as if she were a witness in the box. When he had exhausted her memory he fell silent. Whenever the wind whispered the lights far below seemed to flicker. In his dark corner he chuckled to himself, his only comment, at that stage, a contemptuous:

"He has no such woman."

"Poor Walter! He has to pretend."

"The man is a goose. Dammit, he ought to know the world better by now. He's old enough!"

"You don't need to be so cruel."

She was the goose. She should not have come. Sullenly from his corner he had said:

"So you have allotted two dinners to him and only one to me?"

If he had said it in simple disappointment she might have presumed affection — not when he said it sulkily, superbly self-concerned, out of the hurt vanity of a young man. She had drawn her coat around her neck, felt all her years, asked him quietly:

"How old are you, Giorgio?"

"I told you." Crossly. "Twenty-five. Why?"

"Does one dinner more or less with me mean so very much to you?"

"It could be a test of how much you love me."

"And how much do you love me, Giorgio? And in what sense, Giorgio, do you love me?"

From his corner, in a very loud voice, as if he had been asked if he liked *risotto*:

"Very much. In every sense. After Milano you should know that." Then his tone had suddenly changed, softened, deepened: "I don't know when I met anybody I liked more than you. I'd marry you like a shot if I could."

"And are you married, Giorgio?" — wanly.

In a furious, sarcastic mutter:

"My mother has other plans for me."

"So the Contessa Rinaldi is not good enough for the Countess of Boyne!"

At this he had laughed gaily. It was one reason why she liked him so much: his moods could change like the wind scurrying over the surface of a lake. He said:

"I do wish you would understand the way things really happen in this world. It's got nothing to do with your not being good enough. It's simply that you are broke. As a matter of fact my mother has a great admiration for you. From her point of view it's wholly to your credit that you should have been born in that filthy old pub at Coomagara. Why, she holds you up to me as a model of what *can* be done with nothing. She says you are a spirited and clever woman. But you don't know how tough she is. And she's inquisitive as a hen. That time we met you on the Lakes she went snooping all around the hotel trying to find out about you and Rinaldi. It wasn't difficult. One night at dinner, on the terrace — all those little lamps, the full moon on the lake, the little steamer floating by with its dance music — after the three of us had passed your table, bowing, she shook out her napkin, and whispered to my father and me, like the damned old witch she is, 'My dears, I've just had the most interesting talk with that tall old lady from Milan. She knows the Rinaldis intimately. They are completely on the rocks, just as poor as we are.' "

"Why did she spy on us?"

"Because she saw I was keen on you, of course. Why else?"

"And are you really so poor?" she had asked dully.

"My mother says she's going to turn Castle Boyne into a guesthouse for rich Americans."

"So that's that?"

"That's that, my dear!"

She had looked across at him, immobile, glaring out over the lighted dashboard at the lights of Dublin.

"Giorgio, are you wondering if I'm wondering whether your story is true or not?"

"It's all too true!"

"Giorgio, tell me. What is your chosen bride like? My coloring? A bit younger? My figure? Lived abroad? Went to —"

"Stop it! She's no age, no figure, no coloring. We have never seen her. My mother says she will be one of the rich Americans."

She had shivered with pity for him, and said:

"Let's go and dance somewhere. The cold of death is in my bones."

So they had come down here to this obscure little supper-and-dancing place, somewhere off the windy quays, so dimly lit she could not decipher the travel posters on the walls. They could barely see one another. Now and again other couples would appear out of the dusk on the tiny floor, but there was no telling how few or how many other people were there. They danced to the radiogram. Once she said, "Do you like this place?" He said, "No, but what else is there to do?" They ordered *risotto*. He had brandies; to save his pocket she drank beer. She knew he was in his wicked mood when he said, "These are Italian travel posters. I believe one of them invites us all to come to Bergamo."

It was after his third brandy that he had leaned over the lamp and cackled:

"Molly, are you really so utterly innocent that you don't know what Walter Hunter is after?"

And then he told her, and she refused to believe him until he beat her down and down. When he saw her in tears he bade her airily not to cry — she could still accept her old beau. Her protestations became feebler and feebler. She surrendered only when he asked her if she had been making it all up, "to encourage the others."

She leaned back to survey him, in all three of them, the ridiculous lurches of love.

"I suppose," she said sadly, "you don't realize that you are trying to bully me, Giorgio. But why should you care? You're as good as betrothed to an American from Minneapolis."

"I do care!" he cried back at her.

"Yet you want me to marry Walter Hunter?"

"I want you to marry nobody but me."

She was so astonished by his tone that she snatched the red shade off the lamp. In the naked light his face was transformed. He looked about seventeen, his mouth melting, his eyes misted. Furiously he snatched the shade from her and restored the ruby dusk. There was a prolonged silence, except for the slither of dance shoes and the staccato hiss of a gourd in a Cuban thrum. She collected her bag and gloves:

"I wish I were rich. Innocent child that you are! Let's go. The night is finished."

"One more dance?"

They did not dance it Cuban-way. They held one another very tight. He made her feel like a mother with a child. Then he called the waiter, fumbled with the bill and his pocketbook, said brusquely to her, "I haven't enough, can you lend me a quid?" She did not dare not take the change from him. They walked back arm in arm across the river, around the locked-up Green. Down here in the plain the wind was slight. The stars were out in their legions. In the empty foyer of the hotel he said:

"I suppose I've cooked my goose with you now?"

"There wasn't any goose, Giorgio," she said fondly, and bent her cheek to be kissed. "Only a little *poussin*. Sleep well."

"I'm not going to sleep. It's a fine night for driving. I'll be home in time to see the morning coming up over your little Bergamo. Have a nice breakfast with old Wally."

She did not sleep until late morning. Her shame kept her awake, and the image of that young face, lean, sensitive, cruel, greedy, madcap, enchanting, lovable, staring through the headlights fleeing before him. She kept turning and twisting in her bed and in her mind away from thoughts of Walter Hunter. It would be a refuge. All her worldly wisdom told her it would be a sensible and interesting and dangerous refuge. So close to George. With his rich American wife? Dear Giorgio!

6

Tired from his long drive, he did not wake until late morning. When he was about to go downstairs he found an envelope angled under his door. It contained a sheet of hotel note paper bearing a message from her. *Dear Walter, If you are free for lunch do join me in the foyer at noon. I shall be alone. Molly.* He hastened down. She looked up at him with a wan smile.

"This is delightful, Molly! But you said you were lunching with the Killeens?"

"I decided not to go."

"Our dinner tonight is all right?" he asked.

"We must make it lunch instead, Walter. I cannot dine with you tonight. I am flying to Milan. Let's go into lunch at once, shall we?"

He followed her, aghast. He sat on the edge of his chair, he fiddled with his knife, he stared at her, he told the waiter they did not wish to drink, he called him back.

"Yes, drinks, please," he panted. "Molly? Champagne?"

"Please, Walter!" she groaned. "Not champagne!"

"Two Martinis."

He glared at her blankly. All his carefully prepared words had flown away like escaped pigeons.

"And tomorrow night, too? Is that dinner gone, too?" He was getting more and more angry. "Really, this is too bad of you, Molly!"

She could only open her palms and smile sadly. She saw that he was so upset that he was liable to say the first thing that came into his head, and to her dismay, she found that his anger and his misery made him more *simpatico* than she had ever found him before.

"Molly!" he barked. At once he said, "Sorry!" and laughed, and then coughed, and said, "I had a wonderful night last night. I dined alone. At the Yacht Club."

She looked at her hands. Was she expected to ask, Why wonderful? She looked up. He became aware of her pallor. Her eyes were tired, as if she, too, had not slept. It gave her, as on that night of summer rain in Rome, the vanishing beauty of a peach ripened to the full point when it ought to be picked and eaten at once. He said, in a little voice — strange and rather touching to her in a man so broad, big and ruddy:

"You are pale, Molly. It makes you even more beautiful."

She smiled feebly at the compliment.

"I didn't sleep very well."

"I did not sleep at all. I drove all the way down to Cork after dinner. And back again."

She closed her eyes. He too? This, she thought, is one of those things I will laugh at when I am an old woman.

"Rather a long drive," she said flatly.

"It was after six before I got back. But I didn't mind. I was thinking of the woman I love. From the hill above Saggart I saw the morning sun spreading over Dublin. I was thinking of her, asleep. Her hair strewn on the pillow."

His pigeons were circling, sinking, coming back to him. His eyes began to glow. Any minute now, she felt, he will come to it. They picked at random from the outsize menu. He lifted his glass.

"You know," he said, more at his ease now, "the only times I ever saw you alone you looked pale, lovely, and unhappy."

"Alone?" she asked, startled.

"Alone, I mean, since we were students. Yesterday. Now. That wet night in Rome. The first time was in Turin."

"We never met in Turin."

He leaned forward.

"I did not say met, I said saw. It was in 'Forty-six. Just after the war. I had gone up to Cervinia for the skiing . . ."

He went bit by bit through his story. With apprehension

he noted that she paid no attention to the omelet that had been placed before her. She was staring fixedly through the muslin curtains at the Green. By the time he said, "They were playing *La Sonnambula,*" he saw, with puzzlement, that her eyes were tear-covered. At the end, when he said, "You walked out on the stage and I nearly died," she looked straight at him through the water of her tears.

"And you were actually there all the time! Why on earth didn't you come around afterwards?"

They stared at one another; she waiting for his answer, he gaping at her because he no longer knew the answer. His secret image of her had vanished. Rapidly, as if he were racing backwards after it, he tried to re-create the night, talked of the music act by act, of her songs, of her singing, the lighting, the last falling curtain.

"Walter, you know it so well! And you are so right about that night in Turin. It was one of the best performances I ever gave. As I have good reason to know. But why did you never tell me all this?"

He saw himself in that café, waiting for the train at two in the morning.

"I don't know," he gasped. "I was so lonely! And I was so happy!"

She threw up her chin and she laughed the strangest laugh, a laugh like a breaking wave, curling and breaking between pride and regret.

"I was happy too. If you only knew! I often wonder was I ever quite so happy since. It was that very night, between the acts, in my dressing room, that Rinaldi came in and first told me he was in love with me. Do you remember that enormous bouquet I got at the curtain? Great *reine de joie* roses, straight up from Africa, he had telephoned for them that morning to Milan. They came only just in time, the boy ran with them in his arms, from the taxi, right onto the stage. There were snowflakes on them. They must have cost him the earth. But he was always a spendthrift. No wonder we went broke!" She drew in a deep, passionate, hissing, sobbing breath between her clenched teeth, her eyes swimming, her fists crunched together. "I'm glad we were broke. I'd do it again. It's the only way to live. Not giving a damn."

"And I," he said, "was sitting for hour after hour after the show in a café, drinking, thinking of you, lost in you!"

"Do you know," she raced on, lost in herself, "what we did after the show? You should have been there. Rinaldi invited the whole company to a party at his hotel. He whistled up such a party as you've never seen. Dancing, singing, champagne. And when it was all over, and they were all gone, and now that it's all over forever and all gone forever, I can tell you, Rinaldi and I, left alone . . ."

She hid her screwed-up face in her hands. The sensual picture she evoked sent the blood to his eyes. He stared at her, feeling the first pangs of jealousy, loss, creeping lust. He waited until she was blowing her nose, looking at him self-mockingly, fishing for her compact in her bag, glancing about the restaurant to see if anybody had observed her. She said:

"For two years I kept refusing him. Then I decided that I never would be a great singer." She shrugged. She looked up at him with sudden recollection: "What did you say you did that night?"

He told her again, with bitter feeling. She shook her head.

"What a *salade* we make of our lives!" she sighed.

"So you were unhappy with Rinaldi."

"Unhappy? Who said I was unhappy?"

"You have conveyed it to me in a dozen ways. Molly!" he said intensely, leaning over to her. "Don't try to deceive me. You can't. Don't try to deceive yourself by idealizing him now. You are in the prime of life, your whole life is before you, you can't stop living." He paused. He asked it quietly, but unmistakably: "Would you dare look for happiness again?"

She looked at him for a long while. He hid his trembling hands under the table. She lowered her face in her hands and he saw that her hands, too, were trembling. He leaned back and waited for his fate. When she raised her head and he saw the tears in her eyes again, he knew that he had evoked the one night of all her life that he could never defeat. She said, so softly that he had to lean forward to hear her:

"Walter! Nobody ever finds happiness. We make it, the way people mean when they say, 'Let's make love.' We create it. For all I know we imagine it. We make happiness easily when we are young, because we are full of dreams, and ideals, and visions, and courage. We make our own world that pushes away the other world — your world, and my world, old people's worlds. The young despise the world. Didn't you ever say it when you were young? I'll conquer the world! But you know what happens to us. That little flame in us that could burn up the world when we're young — we sell a little bit of it here, and a little bit of it there, until, in the end, we haven't as much of it left in us as would light a cigarette. And yet," she said, frowning through him, "it is there, to the end. You feel always you might blow on it, make it big again, go on to the very end, without giving up, find the thing, discover the thing, invent the thing, call it anything you like, that you'd always been wanting. Walter, I am not your thing. You are not my thing. I have very little courage left in me, Walter. In fact," she moaned, "I have hardly any left in me at all. That's why I'm flying to Milan tonight. My bags are packed and ready in the hall. Don't come with me."

She grabbed her gloves and her handbag, shook hands with him strongly, and quickly left the restaurant.

In the hotel porch, while her suitcases were being loaded on a taxi, she picked up a colored post card of Saint Stephen's Green, addressed it to The Honorable George Boyne, Ringaskiddy, Co. Cork, and scrawled on it: *I did it well, nobly and virtuously, and you would have thought me a damn fool. I have all my life to wonder if I was. M.* As she stepped into the taxi she saw, down along the wine-red line of Georgian buildings, a gathering of students, girls and boys, outside the University Club, chattering and laughing gaily. She looked at them without envy, slammed the door of the taxi, and drove away.

He let the lace curtain fall. He sat on, sipping a brandy. For the first time in his life he felt the agony that a man suffers in the full awareness of loss. All his senses are alerted a millionfold. His brain burns like a forest fire. And he feels as if the essential parts of his body have been cut out. He saw her hands, her dilated eyes, her convoluted smile. They were not only her hands, eyes and smile but the beauty and desirability of everything unattainable in life. From his pocket he drew out her letter of an hour ago and read it. He saw only the force of her wrist, the strength of her body. He saw her as he had never dared to see her before: those firm calves, the breadth of her hips, her narrow waist, her rich breasts, her yellow pile of hair falling down over her bare body. All this he had lost, as a duelist can lose, forever, as a boxer can lose, forever, as a damned soul loses, forever. This, he knew, he had always wanted. He ordered a brandy, and another, and another, until he was left there alone, seeking for her other image in the round, shining snifter, as one seeks in those toy, round globes that when you shake them give the illusion of falling snow, a tiny figure, remote as a fairy tale, white and virginal, smiling out at him. If he could see her like that, the snow falling silently, the arc lamps fogged by it, the soft thunder in his veins, the music weaving in his memory, he would be happy even though he knew that he would never see her otherwise again. Always the proud, rich, sensual image came before him, smiling, full of love, but not for him.

He gave the young waiter who had been patiently attending him a heavy tip, and went out hatless across the Green to the record shop on Dawson Street. An April shower spattered the shopwindow as he sat in the little booth listening to the *"Ah, non credea mirarti,"* looking out at the falling shower, at the passers-by. The song was as pure as a lark in the clear air. It evoked only the image of a naked Venus. He bought it, went across the street to Doran's pub, from Doran's to the gentle dimness of the empty Buttery, from there to Davy's and from there across to the Bailey. All that afternoon and evening and night he ate nothing. There are in Dublin occasions of vice more squalid by far than in cities that have not been cleaned up. When he reeled out of his last pub late that night, he sought out one of these places, and entered his little season of hell.

He woke up about four in the morning, lying in a lane along the garages and stables at the backs of some houses. He felt a cold mist falling on him. There was congealed blood on his forehead. His pockets were emptied of money. Unheeded, he got back through the empty city to his car outside the hotel, and managed to drive out of the city.

He pulled up on the hill above Saggart and got out to wash himself in a stream.

The rain had stopped. There was Dublin's dish of colored lights below him on the still-dark plain. A cold light touched the underside of the clouds over the Irish Sea. Far away the Bailey lighthouse circled slowly through the pre-morning dusk. He stayed looking over the city and the sea for a long while, watching them slowly become cold and clear, until two sunbeams leaped from below the horizon, a bird threw out a pillar of song, and, as if to its conductor's baton, all the birds at once began to sing like blazes. He closed his eyes and whispered "Christ!" out of the depths of his delight and misery. Then he went back to the car and drove away into the cold wetness of the morning.

Ah, well! Write it off. Write it off to experience.

A dream? Ah, well! It wasn't such a bad dream. If only I hadn't tried to make it become real. Still, isn't this the way most of us spend our lives, waiting for some island or another to rise out of the mist, become cold and clear, and so . . .

Ah, well! It might be a good day after all.

Miracles Don't
Happen Twice

I met Giancarlo on the seafront of Bari late one dank night in November. The Adriatic wind was cold. The waves slapped drearily along the Lungomare. Because of the chilly wind and the gusts of rain only a few people were out of doors, although all Bari loves to gravitate every night to the seafront, enjoying the lights of the cinemas, the big hotels, the fish-vendors' flares, and an occasional boat off-shore luring the fish to the spear with white, down-thrown lamps. I had paused to look with amusement at a travel poster showing the Tower of London as red as wine under an improbably blue English sky. The lights glistened on the raindrops sliding down it. "Yes!" I was thinking. "And I suppose outside Victoria Station the rain is pelting posters of sunny Italy." A voice at my side said:

"*E freddo stasera, signore.*"

He was a little man, with pansy-dark eyes. He was smiling an engaging smile. He wore a raincoat but no hat and he carried a briefcase. One glance at him and I was in no doubt that he belonged to a large and ancient Italian profession. Then, instead of asking me if I wanted a nice girl, he said comfortingly that the sun would shine again tomorrow, and then, in English:

"You are English, *signore?*"

I said "Yes," because I have found in Italy that if I say I come from Ireland either they say, "Ah, yes! The dykes and the windmills!" or else a haze comes over their eyes and I

have to explain that Ireland is an island near England —
which I find a little humiliating and they find disappoint-
ing. Sometimes, when I really want to please them, I choose
to be an American and invent a home in Chicago or Minneapolis.

"I also have been in England," said the little man
eagerly. "My sister lives in England. Near Bournemouth.
Do you know Bournemouth, *signore?* I know it very well.
And Poole. And Eastbourne."

As he chattered on I began to wonder if he were a real
professional. Perhaps he was merely an amateur who
would presently produce picture post cards, cheap coral
brooches or American cigarettes from his little bag, and
would mention girls only if all else failed. I fell into talk
with him willingly. Bari is not an exciting city; the hours
after dinner are the most lonely hours for a traveler; and,
anyway, I have a sympathetic feeling for Italian pimps.
They are not bad fellows. They are a race outside our
world. They do not tempt us. We tempt them. They have
no wish to harm us. They will merely assist us to harm
ourselves if we so desire.

After a while I said, "Let's get out of this beastly wind
and have a drink somewhere," and we began to walk
past the Old Port towards the Corso, talking about Dorset.
But he did not pause at the Corso, for he said kindly: "It is
too expensive here. I know a good place," and led me onward into the dark and winding streets of the old town
away behind the docks, until, in a particularly dark and
narrow alley, we came to a hole in a wall. It was a wine-
shop, arched, empty, brightly lit. There we sat to a trestled
table, over a flask of acrid wine. We were alone.

"And what is your sister working at in England?" I
asked.

"Oh! She is not working," he said proudly. "She is married to a wealthy paper manufacturer."

"Really?" I said, deciding that for tonight I would have to be at least a Sheffield steel king.

"But it is true!" he assured me, instantly interpreting my look. "Veritably true! She went there when she was eleven. Her name then was Federica Peruzzi. Now her name is Mrs. Philpot."

He produced an envelope bearing an English stamp. The dove-gray paper was deckled, embossed with an address in Bournemouth, and signed Federica.

"It happened so," he explained. "After the first war I and my sister were only small children. We lived in Altamura, up in the hills. We had nothing to eat. We came down to Bari because we heard the British navy was in the port." He shrugged and made a face of shame. "We were begging outside the big hotels on the seafront. What else could we do? All I had to sell was one double-almond. As you know, the double-almond brings luck. And," he cried, with a vast, baby-faced smile, "mine brought luck to me. For one night when a sea captain came out of the Grand Hotel I offered him my double-almond. He took it. He looked at me. He looked at my sister. He looked and looked at her. And suddenly he began to weep. '*Signore,*' I said, 'why are you crying?' He took me aside and he began to ask me questions, but he could not take his eyes from my sister. I was very troubled for her. I was only fourteen, and in Altamura they had said that we should find the big world in the valley a very wicked place."

Giancarlo wriggled apologetically with his whole body.

"You see, I loved my little sister, and she was only eleven. But the captain soon explained. His name was Captain Edgeworth. He had lost his only child during the war,

and he said that Federica was the living image of his
Gladys who had died. And as he said this he became sad
and wept again. I knew then that he was an honest man."

"The captain gave me fifty lire and told us both to be at
the hotel again the next morning at ten o'clock. Oh! What
a meal we had that night! It is thirty-four years ago and
never since have I eaten a better meal. Never, never, never
as long as I live will I forget that meal. All night Federica
could not sleep. She kept waking me up and crying out,
'Giancarlo! Our fortunes are made! The rich Englishman
will take care of us for the rest of our lives.' But I said,
'Sleep, little one. We shall never see the captain again. Let
us be content with our fifty lire.'"

Clearly, so far, a true story. Those cries of hope were not
invented. They could only have come out of the old Italian belief in magic, miracles, the wheel of fortune, the
Totocalcio (their football pools), in short, some *deus ex
machina* who alone can change the hopeless reality of life.

"But I was wrong, *signore*. The captain was waiting for
us the next morning. He said, 'Now we go to Altamura.' We
took the train into the hills. He slept that night in the one
bed between me and my father, with Federica asleep at
the tail of it. He ate our poor food, roasted herrings and
dry bread. He trusted me with all his money. I could have
run away with it all, but I did not touch one lire of it. He
arranged between my father and a lawyer to adopt Federica, and to change her name to Edgeworth. The next day
we returned to Bari and he took Federica with him to England. When he died he left her all his money. She met a
Mr. Philpot and married him. Now she has two sons. One
of them was fighting here in Italy during the war."

He drew out his wallet and showed me a crumpled family photograph: two youths, a very lean, English-looking
papa and a middle-aged woman full of Italian fat.

"And you?" I asked. "Did the captain do anything for you?"

"Had I not given up my sister whom I loved? Of course, he gave me money. I traveled a little. I have even been to Rome. I became a valet to a rich American lady in Rome. But I was not happy with her. She was not young and she was not beautiful and she was always trying to make love to me. I could have married her and had all her money, but I was young and romantic, and I wanted real love. Once Federica brought me to Bournemouth. I was unhappy there too. I saw that she did not want me any more. I came back to Bari. I fell in love. I got married."

He removed his raincoat and showed me the tab. It bore the name and address of Burton's in Piccadilly.

"Federica sent me this coat. Sometimes she sends me shirts and shoes. But never any money."

We had some more wine. He asked me about my life. I described to him my two steel factories near Sheffield. He said he was gratified and honored to know me. We talked of his life and with a shrug of self-contempt he gave me a glimpse into his briefcase: brooches of orange-pale coral, picture post cards, American cigarettes. I found that he sometimes gets jobs as a waiter. We talked of the *Totocalcio*. I bought a ticket for him from the *padrone*, and selected the teams, and wrote in his name. As I wrote in his name the sound of the wintry wind outside was one with his deep breathing into my ear.

"It will be lucky," he cried. "I know it! It will win a prize! Will it not, Giacomo?" — turning to the *padrone*, who merely lifted his shoulders and let them fall again. We had some more wine. It was half past eleven before we rose and went out into the wind and the darkness. As he walked down the lane Giancarlo stopped and turned. I was afraid that he was going, at last, to ask me if I wanted a nice girl, and I dearly hoped he would not. When he did not I hoped that I understood why. We had drunk wine together, we had exchanged confidences, we were friends.

Just then the yellow light from a window fell on a dark-haired little girl of about eleven who had come dashing up to him, clasping him about the knees, saying, "Momma is looking for you!" He lifted her into his arms, and kissed her passionately. Then he turned slowly towards me, gazed at me in awe, and whispered:

"This is Federica!" And to her, as if he were showing her the statue of a saint in church: "Little one! This is a rich Englishman who has just arrived in Bari."

For one entranced moment the two of them gazed at me. By the child's wide eyes I knew that she had often heard poppa's fairy tale. For that one moment, in that dark wind-swept alley, I knew what it feels like to be a god in a machine. Then a gust of rain came blasting down on us. I groped in my hip pocket for a note and crumpled it into Giancarlo's fist, gripped his arm, said the hour was late, said my family was waiting for me at my hotel, cried, "*Arivederci!*"

Half an hour later I was lying in the warmth of my bed in the Grand Hotel delle Nazioni. Outside I could hear the sad slapping of the waves on the Lungomare, and the wind, down from the hills of Altamura, softly moaning through the Adriatic night.

No Country for Old Men

1

One morning last September, all the Dublin papers carried headlines like these:

END OF CARNDUFF TRIAL

ONE YEAR FOR COMPANY DIRECTOR

This is how one daily paper reported the conclusion of the odd affair:

At the Belfast Assizes yesterday, sentences of one year and of six months respectively were passed on Joseph Peter Cassidy (sixty-three), described as a manufacturer and company director, and Frederick Robert Wilson (fifty-seven), described as accountant and secretary. Both men gave their address as Boyne Close, County Louth. Cassidy had been charged with the illegal possession of a revolver and six rounds of ammunition, with being a member of an illegal organization, and with entering Northern Ireland by an unrecognized road on the night of July 15th last. Wilson had been charged with membership in an illegal organization and entering Northern Ireland by an unrecognized road on the same date.

In sentencing the accused, Mr. Justice Cantwell said that on the night in question an attack had been made on Carnduff Police Barracks, in the course of which a policeman had been shot dead, and that, after the attack a motor van, the admitted property of Cassidy, had been found only two miles away from Carnduff, its interior heavily stained with blood.

During the trial both defendants insisted that they had no connection whatever with the attack on Carnduff Barracks and that they had entered Northern Ireland on the night in question solely in search of the motor van, which had been removed without permission from the premises of Celtic Corsets, Ltd., of Boyne Close, Drogheda. Cassidy said that he had carried the revolver solely for his own protection.

Mr. Cassidy is a well-known Dublin businessman, a widower with one son, managing director of Celtic Corsets, Ltd., and of Gaelic Gowns, Ltd. Mr. Wilson is secretary to the firm of Celtic Corsets, Ltd., and is unmarried. Both men took part in the 1916 Rising and served side by side in the First Dublin Brigade during the War of Independence.

Both accused have been removed to Crumlin Road Prison, Belfast, to serve their sentences.

The reports in all the other papers were equally short, not to say meager. And yet none of us considered that they should have been more informative. The fact is that whenever perfunctory reports like this appear in the Irish papers we all understand at once that the press is laying a finger on its lips either for political reasons or religious reasons or through a sense of personal delicacy. We guess that some decent man is in trouble, or that some unfortunate priest has gone off the rails, or that some public man has been caught, as the Americans say so vulgarly, with his pants down. We approve of this reserve, this proper regard for human feelings, this *gentillesse* (as the French say), because we Irish have a certain hidalgo quality about us. And, anyway, it might be our turn tomorrow. So we draw a seemly cloak of public reticence over the matter, and then — in whatever golf club, or yacht club, or restaurant or pub the characters in question have been accustomed to frequent — we tap the old grapevine to find out what these fellows have been up to. Over the malt we pass our own judgment on them in seemly privacy.

We certainly had to pursue this Carnduff affair beyond public report and private rumor. We all knew quite well that Joe Cassidy is far too cagey to become a member of any illegal organization at his age and with his income. We know him for a sound, law-abiding citizen who has not carried a gun, let alone killed anybody, for at least thirty-five years. We know Freddy Wilson less well, because he left the country nearly thirty years ago, immediately after the Troubles. Nevertheless, those of us who had known him then, or met him since his return to Ireland to work for Joe Cassidy, assured us that if he actually was doing anything illegal in Northern Ireland it was unthinkable that any policeman would catch him doing it.

We found that Joe's only son, Frank, was a member of the Irish Republican Army, and that on that July night it was he who had borrowed the firm's van to take part in a raid across the border. It so happened that when Joe heard about the van he was at a dinner of the Drogheda chapel of the Irish Manufacturers' Social and Patriotic, and his guts being rich of wine, he had become, not unnaturally, incensed against the boy. After all, Frank could just as easily have stolen somebody else's van. Still in his white tie and tails, and full of fire, Joe had jumped into his Jaguar, and with — or so we presumed — Freddy Wilson, he had torn hell-for-leather after the blue van with the pink corset painted on each side of it. Aided by various sympathetic souls along the road, he had picked up the trail and had the good luck to come up with Frank, a bare ten minutes after the raid, across the border, still with the van, trying to get one of his wounded men back to safety. The wounded youth died under their eyes on the side of the road. The rest was easy to imagine.

Joe and Freddy had sent the son racing back across the border in the Jaguar. They then took over the van and the dead boy. We took off our hats to Joe Cassidy and Freddy Wilson and we let it be known to them both that there would be a public dinner at the Dolphin waiting for them when they came out of jail.

But as the months went by some more details leaked out. For one thing, Freddy had not been with Joe in the Jaguar. Freddy had been in the van with Frank. He had forced Joe's son to take him with him on the raid across the border because he was taking French leave of Celtic Corsets, Ltd., with four thousand pounds' worth of bearer bonds belonging to his old comrade-in-arms in his breast pocket. And he might have got away with them if he had not had the bravado to leave a taunting farewell message to Joe behind him.

The rest was true enough. Joe and Freddy had persuaded Frank to take the Jaguar while they stayed with the van. There they were, then, with a dead youth on their hands, at about one o'clock in the morning, only a mile away from a police barracks that had been attacked by bomb and machine-gun fire ten minutes before . . .

2

Joe waited until he heard the Jaguar driving rapidly away. Then he ran back to the fork of the road as fast as his great bulk and the thin pumps he was wearing would allow. As he ran he could hear nothing but the sound of his own panting and the patter of his pumps on the road. He had no torch, so when he came to the fork he snapped on his petrol lighter and by its fitful light he began shuffling through the long grass, bending, peering, groping, and cursing. He could see nothing except the grass until a beam of light from behind his back showed him the staring face of the dead young man at his feet.

"Found him?" Freddy's voice said from behind the beam.

"The bastards!" Joe said. "We've got to get him into the van and across the border at once. Bring up the van!"

Freddy turned and ran for the van. While he waited for him to return, Joe clambered up on the ditch and saw, a mile away, the kangaroo jumps of the Jaguar's lights making towards the south. He looked left and saw Freddy's lights coming up the road. Then, still farther left, or northward, he saw a third set of lights moving towards the east. The moon was rising and it made the trees against it look very black. Then they were lifting the dead youth, laying him into the back of the van, and Freddy was driving back the way they had come. As he drove Freddy said:

"Did you see the lights of a car away there to the north? It may only be a private car on the main road from Newtown Butler to Clones, but if we are still in the North they may be police or B Specials trying to cut us off. Damnation! I wish I knew to hell where exactly our wandering border is tonight."

They took a right turn. The headlights likewise turned and moved parallel to them on their left.

"I don't like this at all," Freddy said. "See that?" he shouted, and Joe saw what he meant.

It was a letter box inset into a wall, painted in English red. They were still in the North.

When they came to a T-sign they were aware of the other car's lights, now not more than a quarter of a mile to the east. Freddy whirled west, curved under a railway bridge, tore into sixty on the straight, and let out a cry of joy. His headlights had picked up a tattered Southern tricolor hanging from the branch of a tree: they had crossed the border already. He came to a fork, pulled up, turned off his engine, and they both looked back and listened. The lights of the pursuing car were halted about half a mile behind them. They could hear its engine humming in the still summer night.

"This is all very well," Joe said. "We're in the South now. But this bloody border loops all over the place. Any road we take, if we take it far enough, might take us back into trouble again. We had better go very carefully, Freddy-boy!"

Freddy let in the gears and sneaked slowly along the road. The lights behind them moved slowly against distant treetops. Freddy pulled up. The lights whirled and vanished.

"I'm afraid to go on. I expect they have a transmitter."

He got out and climbed the ditch, followed by Joe. He pointed:

"See that? They're going south! I know what's happened. This road must cross a pocket of the South enclosed by two pincers of the North. They're going down the eastern leg of the pocket to cut us off there if we try to cross it."

"Then," Joe said, "let's run across the western leg and get out that way."

"You can bet your last bullet they have a patrol down that way already."

"Then we're boxed!" said Joe. "Have we a map?"

"No! But I see a cottage. I'm going to take a chance on it. We must have a guide."

"What the hell is the good of a guide if there's no road out of this pocket?"

"We can walk across the fields, can't we? But" — and Freddy nodded his head towards the back of the van, questioningly.

Joe looked into the dark maw behind him.

"We'll carry him. I'm not going to let those bastards get him. Once they identify him, all his relations up here will be in the soup."

They got out and knocked at the door of the long, slate-roofed cottage. There was no sound from inside it. They knocked again several times, but they could not hear as much as the sound of breathing from inside. To Joe's surprise, a gun appeared in Freddy's hand. It was that rather old-fashioned type of long-nosed automatic known as a Peter the Painter. Joe knew this type of gun well; he had always carried a Peter the Painter in the old days. As his eye fell on it he remembered in a flash one night when it jammed during a raid in Clanbrassil Street and he would have been a gone man if Freddy had not shot the Black and Tan who was firing at him. Before he could say anything, Freddy had pushed in a pane of glass with the point of his gun and shouted through the hole:

"This is the I.R.A. There's six of us. If you don't come out we'll burn you out. We'll give you one minute."

After a few seconds they heard a slight noise, and then a man's voice said:

"Come to the door."

"No tricks!" Freddy shouted. "We'll shoot!"

They heard a sound of footsteps, and something like a tin basin falling on a stone floor and rotating noisily to rest. A pale glimmer of light appeared to pass the window. A chain rattled and the door opened on the chain, a device Freddy had never in his life seen in any part of the country, even during the Troubles years ago, when he had often been out at all hours of the night in the loneliest mountainy places behind Dublin. His torch showed the face of a pale but unfrightened middle-aged man looking out through the three-inch opening. Impressed by the man's steady look, he said more quietly than he had intended:

"All we want is a guide. We've lost our way and we want to get back on foot across the border."

"No!" the man said sturdily. "I'm not going to help you. This may be the South, but a heap of my neighbors are Orangemen. I do a lot of work with folk across the border." His eye fell on the long-nosed gun. "Of course," he went on amiably, "if you were to as much as point your gun at me . . ."

Freddy grinned with relief. "Consider it done," he said.

"You must do it so that I can honestly swear that you did do it."

Freddy raised the revolver. For good measure he said cheerfully:

"If you don't help us I'll shoot you where you stand."

"Wait until I tell the missus and get me boots on. And put out the lights of yon car. We can take no chances."

Three minutes later the three of them were back in the van. Their guide made no comment on the fact that they were only two and that one of them was in evening clothes. He did observe dryly that they were mighty old to be in the I.R.A. To this Freddy replied:

"We're two brigadier generals. Did you hear the racket our lads made tonight?"

"I heard something like firing in the direction of Carnduff about half an hour ago. And I saw a rocket going up from over thereabouts about twenty minutes back."

"Twenty minutes! No wonder the patrols are out."

They drove slowly, in silence and moonlit darkness, until they came to a fork where they turned south and came to a railway bridge. Freddy was silent because he was aware of the presence of danger; the man was silent because he was a Northerner; and Joe was silent because he was thinking about that gun. After driving for what seemed to Freddy like a long mile, the man at his side told him they must now abandon the van and walk the rest. Even when they opened the van doors and lifted out the dead young man he said nothing, only stooping to look into the blankly staring eyes, shaking his head partly from pity and partly to indicate that he did not recognize him. The three of them carried the body south along the track. It was slow walking, and when he halted them and assured them they had not covered a quarter-mile their aging bones could not believe him. He whispered:

"I'm going to leave ye now. If ye followed this road or yon railway line any farther ye'd find yeerselves back inside the border. From this on ye'll have to take to the fields. Go in a straight line with yon red star foreninst ye. After about half a mile or so ye'll pass out through our Gap o' the North. The Gap's not much more than a quarter-mile wide down there, but ye can't miss it if ye remark that it lies between a wide copse of beeches on the west and a low grassy hill on the east. Carry on then and it'll maybe be another half-mile before ye come to a wee road. Ye'll be well into the South by then. That road will take ye fair and free anywhere ye like in the Republic."

They looked ahead of them into the level darkness. The sky was white with stars. In the clear summer sky the moon was now as big and bright as a tin basin. They saw no lights on the plain. They heard no least sound. Freddy whispered:

"Is there any danger that the Specials, if they're out, would cross the Gap to stop us?"

"Every danger! They'd follow a man twenty miles into the Republic if their blood was up. And it'll be up the night. Ye'll have to move slowly and quietly and take no chances. I can do no more for ye. God bless ye! And don't make a sound. D'ye hear that dog?"

They heard a dog barking.

"That dog must be three miles away."

When they looked around again he had vanished as if he had been a ghost or a leprechaun.

When he had vanished they sat to rest with the dead youth between them on the grass. Joe whispered that that was a fine Irishman and when, if ever, they got safe home he'd send his wife a present of half a dozen Celtic Corsets. They dared not smoke. On a clear night like this the glow of a cigarette would be seen a mile off. The low barking of the distant dog went on baying the moon. Freddy was bending over the nameless youth, looking at him by the light of the moon. The blank eyes stared at the sky. The hair was dark and glossy. The nose was broad with wide nostrils. The open mouth showed fine white teeth smiling at them.

"Do you remember Harry de Lacey?" he whispered back to Joe. "He was killed in that ambush at Finglas in Nineteen-twenty. This lad is very like him."

Joe leaned over to look.

"He's not unlike," he whispered. "I met Harry's brother Tony only the other day. He has a job in the Dublin Corporation."

"We don't even know this lad's name," Freddy whispered. "We ought to search him. If we're caught or have to run for it we don't want to leave anything on him that would identify him."

They went through the youth's pockets. He was carrying a heavy Webley forty-five and six spare rounds. Joe thought of Freddy's Peter the Painter and quickly pocketed the Webley and the bullets. Between them they collected a cheap pocketbook, some papers, a pale-blue handkerchief, a full packet of cigarettes, matches, a few coins, a door key, a hair comb, a fountain pen, a gardener's pruning knife, rosary beads and his wristlet watch. Since they dared not light a match to look at the papers or the pocketbook, and the moonlight was not bright enough to read them, they wrapped the lot in the blue handkerchief and buried it carefully under some loose stones directly at the foot of a stanchion wire from one of the telegraph poles along the railway embankment. Then Freddy took a line between a near, lone tree, a copse beyond it, and the red star, and they staggered off, carrying the corpse between them by the armpits and the legs.

It was heavy going, and they advanced very slowly, listening carefully, breathing heavily, resting many times — they were not young and a body is dead weight — and always laying the corpse between them on the dew-wet ground. During the first panting pause Joe tore off his stiff collar and black tie and whispered from where he lay on his back to Freddy, also strewn supine beside him on the grass:

"Where did you get that Peter the Painter?"

"I've had it by me for thirty-five years."

"If we're challenged will you fire?"

"To the last bullet, damn them!"

"Good man!" Joe whispered.

Freddy was sitting up in angry surprise.

"Did you doubt it? You don't think I'm going to do five years in jail in Belfast for this?"

Joe hesitated and then said apologetically: "I wouldn't have asked you in the old days. But we're not as young as we were."

Freddy lay back. He was silent for a while. Then, softly, he uttered his thoughts, not so much to the ear beside him as to the stars above him:

"I don't blame you. When a man starts to grow away from his youth he gets fond of the world. But you forget that when we grow older still we begin to get sick of it! Dying would be easy now, Joe!"

"Yes?"

"Did you ever read Faust?" Freddy whispered.

"I saw the opera once or twice, at the Gaiety."

"The opera is no good! They always make Faust an old fellow with white whiskers. That's not true to life. An old bucko like that wouldn't give a damn about being young again. Not after philosophic wisdom came to him. I've read everything about Faust I could lay my hands on. I used to think one time that it was wrong for Goethe to make Faust ruin that girl. I used to think that if Faust was a magician and had all that magical power he should have been able

to have any girl without ruining her. As I got older I realized how true it was. It's the whole point of the story.
There's no magic strong enough to cheat the world. It was
right to make the world, the flesh, and the devil cheat him
in the end."

"There's no such thing as magic!" Joe murmured smugly.

Freddy laughed softly and bitterly.

"I studied that subject very carefully the time I had a
tricks and jokes shop in Manchester. I studied white magic
and black magic. I studied telepathy, and hypnotism, and
spiritualism. I even studied the Black Mass." He chuckled
quietly. "One time during the war I drew circles on the
floor of the shop with chalk, late at night. All the city was
under the blackout, and nobody in the streets but the fire-
wardens. Suddenly all the air-raid sirens began to wail.
Then the only sound was the bombs and the ack-ack. I
raised my voice and I called up the devil. The next second the whole block next to ours went up with a bang. Do
you believe in the devil?"

"Oh, well!" Joe laughed, evading carefully, as if he did
not wish to antagonize anybody. "But not with horns and
a tail, of course!"

"He's there," Freddy whispered. "The whole world's a
juke box full of his little whiney tunes. You can buy them
from him the way you could have bought my tricks and
jokes from me. You don't know what I'm talking about!
You're too bloody stupid." He paused and said apologetically: "I'm trying to explain to you why I tried to steal
your bearer bonds tonight."

"Forget it," said Joe. "For the time being," he added
hastily.

"I wasn't able to do it," Freddy said, "because you are
a better gangster than me."

He sat straight up and looked down at the youth's face

staring at the stars. Joe sat up too. As if still thinking of the devil he whispered:

"I never did any harm to anyone."

"Apart from existing!"

"I go to confession and Communion every first Friday of the month. I go every year of my life to Lough Derg. That's no joke of a pilgrimage. Three nights fasting and walking on the cold stones. I was often wet to the skin, kneeling in the rain. That ought to help me when my hour comes."

"I'm a poor sort of Christian," Freddy said. "If I ever was one."

"You ought to do Lough Derg," Joe advised him fraternally. "I'm going to do Lough Derg if I get safe out of this bloody kip-o'-the-reel." He took out the Webley and broke it open. "Begod," he whispered, "he's after firing every bloody round in this!"

He started to eject the spent rounds and reload the chambers.

"That's the ticket," Freddy murmured, watching him. "Always back for a win or a place. Put your trust in God but keep your powder dry. Leave us be going. It's near two o'clock. The sun will be up soon after four."

All over the land there were long, thick swaths of moonlit mist, so that when each took his turn at carrying the dead youth on his back he looked like a giant walking through milk. In this way they moved a bit faster, but Freddy had to halt many times because Joe's knee began to pain him badly, so that he limped and groaned even when he was walking unburthened. His stiff shirt was crumpled like an old sail. His thin streaks of gray hair halved his big rosy turnip of a head. His ruddy face was wet with perspiration. His light shoes were soon soaked with the heavy dew and muddy from a swampy patch on

which they chanced in the darkness. During one of their
pauses to rest he whispered, looking at the anonymous
face looking up beyond him at the studded sky:

"Was it all a waste?"

"He died young," Freddy said enviously. "Bliss was it in
that dawn . . . People envy us, too. They say we had the
dawn, and the whole day after it. Now every day is either
a year long or it has only a couple of hours in it."

And he suddenly thought, in fright, of all the hosts of
young men who were killed in the wars of Europe, more of
them than the hosts of visible and invisible stars overhead,
and he felt that death is always a waste.

"I wasn't thinking of him," Joe whispered. "I was thinking of us and all we did in our time."

"Yah!" Freddy mocked, mocking his own last thought.
"Time is an old man's thought. When you're young you
don't need clocks or watches. You measure things by Now.
For dogs and boys it's always Now. A Now that lasts forever. Do you remember the long summer days when you
were young? Endless! That's because when you're young
you're not killing yourself by thinking. You're just doing
and living, without an atom of consciousness of the wonder
of what you're squandering. 'That is no country for old
men. The young in one another's arms . . .' Even death
is lovely when you're young. But it's a terrible and lonely
thing to look at the face of death when you're young. It
unfits you for the long humiliation of life. Aye! When a
man stops living he starts watching the end of the sand-
glass dripping to tell him that his egg is cooked. Did you
ever examine your conscience, Joe?"

Joe started.

"My conscience? I examine it every month when I go to
confession."

"That's where time and age get a hold of you. They remind you that sooner or later you'll have to set your sail and float out to sea. But you don't know what I'm talking about — you haven't got a conscience."

"I know right from wrong," Joe said warmly. "More than you do! What were you trying to do tonight with my bearer bonds?"

Freddy ignored him. He said coldly:

"We are a childish people. As childish as a boy with his first catapult, or an old stone in a river-bed."

Joe said, "Aye!" indifferently and placatingly. He was thinking what a lunatic he had been to bring this lunatic back to Ireland to work for him.

"You know something, Joe? This country was made for young people. Nobody else but them can live in it, or die in it. Look at you and me! We can neither live in it nor die in it. This country is a cheat of a country for old men, that's why all the old men in this country are cheats — cheating the cheat! Look at us tonight. Why don't the bloody British military or the bloody black-coated bobbies or the flaming B Specials come and give us a chance now to fight them and die decent? But — no! They won't. Another bloody cheat! We're not even allowed to die! All we can do is go creeping around eating, and drinking, and blathering and cheating, and making money, and getting old and withered, and beating our breasts like you, you dying sow, up in Lough Derg." His voice had been rising all the time. Now he suddenly lifted his head like a dog baying the moon and lifted his two fists to the night and screamed at the top of his voice: "I want to fight! Come out, ye bastards, and fight!"

Joe grabbed him and clasped a hand over his mouth.

"For Christ's sake!" he growled. "Are ye mad? Do you want them to catch *him*?"

Freddy bowed his head. Then he lifted it and shook it

sadly. His calm was as sudden as his storm. He whispered:
"You see? You're caught, even through the dead. I tell
you it's only the young who can die well, because they're
proud and ignorant and lovely." He leaned over and
brushed away a tender-legged spider from the young man's
pallid brow. "We lost his hat," he observed. "Some ould
lad will find it and wear it. Like a crown. Do I see the
light of a car? Or a window?"

"If you do, you might be seeing the road we're looking
for."

"Come on!"

They struggled on again. Freddy had to do all the carrying now, with the corpse slung backwards loosely over one
shoulder in a sort of fireman's lift. He was wet to his knees.
He squelched at every step. The corpse's head rolled at
every stumble, and its two hanging hands swayed. At the
next pause, after Freddy had laid him softly down, Joe
said, wiping his face and neck:

"Freddy, would you explain one thing to me? Why was
I such a fool as to bring you back here from Manchester?"

Freddy looked ironically at him.

"Because I'm your lost youth. I'm your lost faith. You
can never stop remembering the time when you were
young and slim, like this poor devil here, when you felt immortal, when you felt grand, when you felt the lord of the
world. And you can never understand why you stopped
feeling like that. So you wanted to have me around to see
how was I handling your problem."

"Freddy, why was it that when we were young and trying to die for Ireland we all felt immortal?"

"Because time meant nothing to us. I've explained all
that to you, you big ballox!"

"We were like angels," Joe whispered, filled with awe.

"With flaming swords!"

"And now," said Joe, bitterly, "I'm selling women's corsets."

They lay on the grass, the dead boy between them, all three staring up. A star streaked across the sky, exploded and vanished. At long last Joe said, so gently that Freddy barely heard him: "You called me a gangster a minute ago. Well, I was one, and I'm not ashamed of it."

Freddy, supine and silent, stared upward at the lofty white ball of the moon. After a while:

"That isn't correct. We *are* gangsters now. But we weren't always. We were killers. In every revolution there have to be killers. But there also have to be men who sanctify the killing. They make it holy, and beautiful, and splendid and glorious. We had a lot of men like that in Ireland once, and as long as we had them life was worth killing. They gave us a faith. Now we're killers still, but there's nobody to kill now so we've gone into business. We use the word in business — 'A wonderful killing.' "

His eyes focused away from the moon towards the pale blue flowers beside him that were bright even in death. He went on:

"Joe! I'm sick of hearing you talking about all you're trying to do now for Ireland. It won't work. Nothing on God's earth could make corsets holy, or beautiful, or splendid or glorious."

After a while he became aware that Joe was crying. After another while Joe said:

"If any of the fellows in the Dolphin saw me now they'd think me mad."

"They're usually mad enough to think you're sane," Freddy said, and they scrambled up again.

The next time they rested they were sitting back to back by a mossy rock protruding from the stubble of a cut meadow. Joe said sourly:

"A bloody tricks and jokes shop! So that's what you were doing all those years in Manchester? Were you down to that?"

Freddy snorted.

"When I left Ireland in 'Twenty-two I hadn't as much as a penny piece. I was the dis-bloody-well-illusioned revolutionary. Even to think of Ireland made me puke what I never ate. I was so low that first year in Manchester that if I took one step up I'd be in the gutter. I had no skill. I was just a smarty. I met a widow whose husband used to run a tricks and jokes shop; you know the sort of thing — false noses, imitation ink blobs, stink bombs, card tricks, little Celluloid babies that squirt water when you squash 'em, nutcrackers in the shape of a woman's legs, drinking glasses that leak down your shirt front when you use them, cockroaches to drop in a fellow's beer. A cozy little place. With a cozy little room behind the shop. On winter nights, after we put up the shuts, with the soft pink web of Lancashire mist down over the city, we'd sit on each side of the little red eye of the cooking range. Liz would be reading the *Evening Chronicle* — she always preferred it to the *News* for some reason. She'd say, 'Freddy, wot abaht comin' to see Clark Guyble in *Hearts Aflyme?*' I wouldn't go. I'd be reading a book about Irish history, or thinking, 'What is it like tonight in Dublin?' She never knew what I was thinking. She'd say, 'Wot are you thinking abaht?' I'd say, 'Some new trick.' I used to deceive her nearly every night of the year. We lived together for eighteen years. She was killed in the blitz. I found her stark naked in the rubble, sliced in two."

He half slewed around to Joe. Joe turned to him. He went on:

"While you, you big sow, were here in Ireland, getting fatter and fatter, making corsets with designs from the

Lindisfarne Gospels on 'em. I wrote to you for help twice. Did you answer me? Did you, you cur?"

"I was working for Ireland," Joe protested. "Building up the country we fought for."

Freddy took out his Peter the Painter and began to wipe it in his handkerchief. Joe felt in his tails for the Webley.

"That looks very like my old Peter the Painter," he said.

"It is! I took it with me to Manchester after the Troubles and the Treaty. In memory of the old days when we were all boys together."

Joe faced him, full of joy.

"Did you really? All those years?"

Freddy slipped off the safety catch of the Peter the Painter. His forefinger padded gently on the trigger. His left hand felt for the bulk of the bearer bonds in his breast pocket. Joe gripped the butt of the Webley. Smiling, they faced one another.

"Freddy!" Joe said quickly. "After you left Ireland in 'Twenty-two it was the Civil War, when every man had to choose his side, for the Free State or for the Republic, for De Valera or for Mick Collins. I followed Mick."

"I know it," Freddy smiled. "And it was as well for me that I went to England, for if I'd stayed at home I'd have been for Dev. And you'd have plugged me for it!" he added savagely.

Joe gripped his arm. His voice rose.

"I never killed no Irishman!"

"Maybe you didn't," Freddy agreed, and swayed the gun a little. "All you had to do was to give the orders. 'Is that bastard de Lacey alive yet?' you'd say to one of your pals. And you wouldn't have to say it twice."

He pointed the gun at Joe as if he merely wanted to emphasize the "you."

"Why do you mention that name?" Joe asked in a cold whisper.

"We mentioned it a while ago. But you only mentioned his brother Tony. How well you never mentioned his brother Marky? Marky de Lacey was my best friend, Joe," he said, and stuck the gun into Joe's side. "My best friend! And he was found up on the Three Rock Mountain with a hole in his skull. Don't you ever think of him, Joe, when you're up in Lough Derg praying for your rotten carcass? Don't you ever once think of Marky de Lacey?"

Joe's hand made a backward movement, but Freddy stuck his gun barrel deeper into his fat. Joe's voice rose higher still.

"I never laid a wet finger on Marky de Lacey!"

"Oho!" Freddy sighed. "Wasn't it well for me I went to England!"

Joe's voice rose to a bat's squeak in the warmth of his protestation:

"Not you, Freddy! Not you! Not you!"

Freddy peered at the dark outline of his turnip head and saw the faint starlit shine on the sweat of his temples and he saw the two eyes glowing like a cat's at him. He withdrew the gun.

"Hell roast yeh," he said exhaustedly. "If you say so I have to believe you."

"I do say so, Freddy. I swear it before God Almighty."

"All right," Freddy agreed wearily. "If you swear it before God Almighty. I suppose I really am your last remaining bit of honesty."

He leaned down and began to brush a stalk of unmown meadowsweet with the long tip of the automatic. He wondered if he should tell Joe why he had really kept it all those years. He decided not to tell, because he did not care any more. He suddenly felt the way a man must feel when he realizes that he has at last become impotent from old age. He clicked on the safety catch. Joe leaned closer to him:

"Freddy, it's what I often wanted to tell you. The real reason why I brought you home was that I wanted to clear up everything with everybody. They say I did things I never did, they put all the blame on me for things other men did, and because I was the boss I had to take the knock, but I never did them. I'd have told you all this years ago only I thought you were another that didn't trust me. It was only when I saw tonight how you kept my old Peter the Painter for old times' sake — and when we're here together helping the young fellows — handing on the torch as you might say — keeping the old flag flyin' — that I knew you'd believe your old pal in the heel of it all."

Freddy looked at the smooth, young face on the grass. He clicked the safety catch off again. He looked at the great, ugly, sweating head leaning over and down to him, and he smelled the smell of fear. In disgust he clicked the safety catch on again. All his hate was gone.

"Oh, well," he said, "if you even only did a tenth of the things they say you did, Lough Derg won't save you. Nor all the fivers you ever gave to old beggarwomen for winter coal. Come on! It'll soon be a new day. Leave us bury him. Leave us bury everything we ever believed in and be shut of them forever."

They got up once more. Lugging the dead boy between them, they struggled on.

The invisible sun was now glowing beyond the level land to their left. Soon the sky over there became a faint fringe of apricot merging into the mauve night retreating across the sky. They crossed another mist-swathed field and came to a low wall which, they found, edged a little road near the junction of three roads. When they climbed over the low wall and laid their burthen on the dew-wet verge, they both tumbled exhausted on the grass.

"We made it," Joe said aloud.

"I'm sorry we did," said Freddy, strewn on his back.

He woke a quarter of an hour later, sat up, and saw a building about five hundred yards up the road, its chimneys standing dark against the bright portion of the sky. In the raw morning light it looked cold and unfriendly. As he got up and walked towards it he suffered a gently pricking pang of realization that he was back in a world so long forgotten that, seen again, it was as unreal as a half-remembered dream. He was looking at a schoolhouse, stone-cut, slated, at least seventy-five years old. He went in through the little iron gate and looked up at the carved plaque on the wall. It was in Irish. They were safely in the South.

Turning around, he saw a cement-faced dwelling house facing the school, all its tawny holland blinds drawn on sleep, its shaggy lawn and draggled flower beds gray with dew. The teacher's house. He looked wider still, oppressed by the intense silence, by the suspension of life, by the half-light; the spread of empty sky and land entered him as an image of Death waiting to enfold his own slight figure alone at its morning edge. He might have been a bather naked by the edge of the sea about to commit himself, to swim out until he could swim no farther. As a youth he would have held out his arms joyously to it, exulting in the adventure. Now, it was not an ocean that invited him; it was just another day. Yet it was also the hour when a man can no longer evade whatever truth he has collected through his life. He felt for his gun again, and as he touched it he felt like a gambler rubbing his last ivory chip between his fingers.

He turned and ran back quickly along the little dusty

road to Joe and he kicked him hard on the rump. Joe
started awake and groaned with stiffness and pain. Freddy
knelt beside him on one knee.

"Joe!" he besought him.

"I'll get rheumatics outa this. I know I will!" Joe said.

"Joe! Leave us go up North for God's sake and let off a
couple of rounds at somebody. We don't want to go home
now, do we? Joe! You bastard! It's our last chance to do
something decent before we die."

"Die?" said Joe, and let out a gasp of pain as the night
scrawled its first revenge on his lumbar regions. "Begod
and I can tell you it would give me the greatest satisfaction
to have a crack at those bastards."

Meaning, Freddy understood miserably, that it would,
in other, more suitable, entirely hypothetical and now quite
historical times and circumstances, have given him the
greatest satisfaction. Freddy clutched his arm.

"Joe!" he sobbed. "For God's sake, Joe!"

"At night sometime?" Joe temporized. "That'd be the
ticket! Eh?"

"Now!" Freddy wailed. "You know damn well that once
you get back to your office and your desk and your appointments book, and all the photographs of yourself all over
the mantelpiece, you'll never do another decent thing to
your dying day."

"It's a pipe dream," Joe sighed, and felt his hip tenderly.
"Our dancing days are done."

Freddy rose up slowly and looked down at him. He
threw his Peter the Painter into a green-coated pool beside the road. He felt his breast pocket and pulled out the
fat, folded envelope containing the bearer bonds. After a
second's hesitation he threw the package into Joe's lap.
Joe put the package in his breast pocket, took out the
Webley, looked at it, glanced mistrustfully at Freddy, and

put it back in his pocket. Freddy sniffed sarcastically. Then he jerked his head towards the schoolhouse.

"That's the schoolteacher's house up the road. We'll carry him up there and hide him there under the fuchsia bushes. Your Frankie can come back tonight and bury him. Then we'll walk on until we meet a car. I could do with a whisky."

Joe was still sitting on the gray-wet grass, his two hands splayed out on either side of him. As he looked up the road his voice took on a touch of its normal daytime hectoring tone:

"Are you quite sure we're in the South?"

"I'm afraid so," Freddy said, as impersonally as any secretary to any manager.

Joe, spread-handed, spread-legged, looked up the road, and sank back even more heavily on his behind. He shook his fat head miserably and clutched his sore knee.

"I'm played out."

"All right. Lie down and rest, you sod! I'll carry it."

"No," Joe snarled. "We carried it together so far. We'll carry it to the end together."

Once more they struggled up the road, bearing the youth between them, Freddy holding him under the knees, Joe holding him under the armpits; a small man in a gray alpaca coat and a big, burly man in tails, white shirt front, no collar. They laid the youth as far in as they could under the fuchsia hedge of the teacher's garden. Two thrushes hopped on the shaggy lawn. The holland blinds did not stir. As Freddy crossed the arms on the chest, a red petal fell on one of the hands and drops of dew sprinkled one cheek. They arranged the branches to hide the body; Joe knelt and recited three Hail Marys, and Freddy, standing, heard himself murmuring the responses as if somebody else were saying them. He was much impressed by the intercession for all sinners at the hour of death. It made him realize that the figure hidden under the flowering shrub was dead. They threw a last glance at the holland blinds and quietly left the garden. Foot-weary, they walked away up the dusty road, heads lowered, a little at a loss at having no burthen to carry, so tired out that they did not advert to the fact that the sunrise was on their right.

Less than half an hour later they were back in the North, facing the guns of a Northern patrol.

Freddy is out now, and back on his job with Celtic Corsets, Ltd. After all, as he says to Joe every week when he visits him in Crumlin Road Prison, Belfast, where else can he go? And who else, as Joe replies, would be fool enough to have him? These weekly visits are ostensibly to discuss business, but the part that Joe really loves — though he pretends modestly to wave it away — is when Freddy draws from his portfolio what they call the Manuscript. It is Joe's biography, which Freddy is composing very carefully and very, very slowly. As he reads the latest couple of pages, the prison walls fade, and Death flowers exquisitely again.